HIS
FANTASY
GIRL

HIS
FANTASY
GIRL

NINA CROFT

Entangled Publishing
644 Shrewsbury Commons Ave
STE 181
Shrewsbury, PA 17361
rights@entangledpublishing.com

Brazen is an imprint of Entangled Publishing, LLC.

Edited by Candace Havens
Cover design by LJ Anderson/Mayhem Cover Creations
Cover art from 123RF

Manufactured in the United States of America

First Edition October 2015

ENTANGLED
BRAZEN

For Rob…my hero.

Prologue

Things to do before you die…

In the distance, the ship burned, listing in the water like the great bloated corpse of some sea monster. The sea had settled, the rage of the storm dying to nothing, and the lifeboat swayed gently in the ebb and flow. Back and forth…

"Oh, shit." Heat washed over him. Logan McCabe slapped his hand over his mouth and lurched to the side of the boat. There was nothing left in his stomach, and he hung there staring down at the dark, treacherous water below.

Never again.

Pushing himself back up, he sank onto the bench seat, eyes narrowing at the looks of amusement directed his way. "I fucking hate boats," he growled, swallowing the sour taste in his mouth. "I'm never going on a goddamn cruise again."

The man sitting to his left let out a short laugh. Vittorio D'Ascensio appeared amazingly cheerful considering it was his multimillion-dollar cruise ship rapidly sinking beneath the Mediterranean. But things could have been much worse. At least everyone was accounted for, and Vito hadn't wanted the ship anyway—he'd been in the process of trying to sell it to Logan when the storm had struck. That's what had brought Logan here. He wanted to expand his business out of nightclubs and had thought a cruise line might be an interesting addition.

Never going to happen.

Vito reached inside his orange life vest and pulled out a silver flask. He offered it to Logan. "I take it the deal's off?"

"Too damn right, the deal's off." Logan unscrewed the lid and took a swallow. The smooth scotch—double malt if he wasn't mistaken; nothing but the best for Vito—flowed down his throat, soothing his stomach. Then the boat rolled again and he clamped his lips closed to stop the scotch coming back. When he was sure he wasn't going to puke again, he took another swig and leaned his head back. "I feel like crap."

"And I thought you were a tough guy, McCabe." The man on his other side held out his hand. Logan handed him the flask and gave him a quick once-over. Josh's face was pale, lines of pain bracketing his mouth, his broken leg stretched out in front of him, held straight by the makeshift splint.

"Well, I was too busy carrying your sorry ass to safety to think about throwing up earlier," Logan replied.

"Yeah, thanks for that."

As head of security for the ship, Josh had found Vito in the chaos, meaning to ensure he got to safety, but the Sicilian had refused to leave until everyone else was away. Logan had battled side-by-side with the two men, directing the last of the passengers off the ship before nearly getting cut off by the flames.

Logan didn't make friends easily; he was a loner at heart, but something about facing death together forged a bond. Once the shock of near death, and the euphoria of actually surviving, had faded, they'd talked. And as they talked, something changed. What started as a joke—things to do before you die—took on a more serious tone. Everyone had regrets. Now, each of them vowed to choose the one big regret of their lives, and after this was over, they would go home and do something about it.

"Come on, McCabe, time to choose," Josh said. "We've told you ours." Josh had a wife he hadn't seen in over five years; he intended to change that.

"Now it's your turn," Vito added. Unlike Josh, Vito had no wife, because his bride-to-be had run out on him mere hours before their wedding. Vito planned on finding out why. "One thing you're going to go back and change."

Logan hugged the blanket around his shoulders and gazed across the sea. Far off to the east, the sun was finally rising, lighting the sky with the new day. The wind had dropped to nothing, and everything had an eerie stillness in the half-light.

Did he have any regrets?

It was so long since he'd seen her. In reality, anyway—even after all these years, she still visited his dreams. He closed his eyes and her image flashed up in his mind. Heart-shaped face, blue eyes, long, mahogany hair. His fantasy girl.

"I had this one-night stand," he started. "Eleven years ago. It was…good." It had been the hottest night of his life. "The next day I was arrested—long story. I spent a year in prison and never saw her again."

But the memory of that one night with her had kept him sane through the horror of prison. He'd thought he was a tough guy and could handle anything, but that first night, when the door clanged shut, locking him in that tiny cell, he'd really believed he might not be tough enough. So he'd pushed away reality and thought about *her* instead, her sweet mouth, her soft breasts, her tight, hot pussy wrapped around his dick. She'd got him through the worst year of his life.

"Every night for that whole year, I'd lie in my bunk, and I'd have these fucking fabulous fantasies about her. She kept me sane."

"You never looked her up?" Josh asked.

He shrugged. "What was the point? I reckoned she'd either be a disappointment or she wouldn't. And if she was as good as I remembered, what the fuck was I supposed to do? I wasn't ready to settle down." Probably never would be. "It was a lose-lose situation, so I didn't even look."

"And now?"

He thought about dying without ever seeing her again. "Now I'm going to go hunt down my fantasy girl. See how those fantasies compare to reality."

The muscles in his belly tightened, and he recognized that he was afraid.

There was no way any real woman could match up to his dreams.

He'd finally have to let her go.

And then what?

Chapter One

Abigail Parker smoothed down the skirt of her gray suit and slipped into her black, low-heeled pumps. A quick glance in the mirror showed she was ready to go. She didn't need to leave for work for an hour yet, but Jenny was due home from school any second and Abby wanted to spend some time with her before she had to go.

These moments were precious, and she always made sure they had some quality time together, whatever shift she was working. The last ten years had been difficult, but Abby was finally getting to where she wanted to be.

The doorbell rang and she headed out of the kitchen and down the hallway.

She opened the door and took an automatic step back. The man standing on the doorstep was tall, nearly a foot taller than her five-foot-four, so she had to crick her neck to look into his face.

She didn't know him…did she?

Surely she'd have remembered.

He was the most stunning man she had ever set eyes on,

his midnight black hair pulled back into a ponytail, revealing sharp cheekbones and silver-gray eyes. The black and red ink of a tattoo edged out of the neckline of his T-shirt, and more snaked down the length of his right arm. He wore black jeans that clung to his long legs and he looked lean and mean and…vaguely familiar. Something about him tweaked at her memory, but she couldn't work out what. She returned her attention to his face. He still hadn't spoken, but was returning her scrutiny, a small frown pulling his brows together as though she wasn't who or what he'd expected.

Then he smiled; a tilt of his sensual lips, and flutters started in her belly. Most unexpected.

"Abigail Parker?" His voice was low and husky, the words a question.

Where had she seen him before? London was a big city, and she met lots of people through her work, but if she could concentrate for a moment it would come to her. At the same time, a little niggle of foreboding suggested perhaps she was better off not remembering. A smile like that could mean nothing but trouble. And she did not do trouble. She never did trouble. She was practical, sensible, and the few dates she did have were with nice men, not tattooed bad boys who only had to smile to melt the panties right off a good girl.

And why was she even thinking about panties melting?

No man had affected her like this. Not ever.

Liar.

Well, okay once. But that was a long time ago and best not thought about.

She returned her attention to his face and found him watching her, one eyebrow raised, and she realized she hadn't answered his question. She licked her lips and wiped her palms down her sides. "*I'm* Abigail Parker."

Midnight black hair. Silver eyes. The dark slash of his brows. *Where* had she seen him before?

"You don't remember me, do you?"

His question dragged her from her thoughts. He sounded a little...pissed off, as though the meeting was not going as planned and he wasn't quite sure how to proceed.

"Should I remember you? Mr....?"

He gave a slightly rueful smile. "I guess not." Faint amusement twinkled in his eyes, and he gave a slight shake of his head. He looked past her into the hallway. "Can I come in?"

Her reaction must have shown in her face because he gave a short laugh. "I take it that's a no." He rubbed a hand over his jawline, faintly shadowed with a day's growth of beard. Something in the movement tweaked a chord in her memory, but the answer stayed just out of reach. "Shit, this is difficult." He took a deep breath. "Okay, so the thing is...we used to know each other."

"We did?" She was getting a really bad feeling, was in fact having to fight the urge to slam the door in his face and run and hide under the bed.

"Well, maybe 'know' isn't the right word." His lips quirked. "Unless we're talking in the biblical sense."

Her mouth dropped open and her eyes stretched wide. "What? No way. I think I would have remembered." But that bad feeling was getting bigger, swelling, and any second now she was guessing it was going to burst all over her.

"It was a long time ago," he said.

No. Freaking. Way.

She wanted to squeeze her eyes tightly shut and put her hands over her ears. Because she knew what was coming next and she didn't want to hear it. And she was suddenly quite aware of why he looked so familiar. Finally, she managed to croak out a question. "How long?"

"Eleven years." He studied her, his head cocked to one side. "I'm guessing it's coming back."

She stared at him—well, at his chest, where his T-shirt strained tight over the swell of muscles. Why? Why was he here after so long? What could he possibly want? Whatever it was, she couldn't deal with it right now.

"Logan McCabe." The name came out as a whisper.

She'd had sex with this man. And multiple orgasms. She was tied to him by tethers he knew nothing about. Did he?

It was weird that she'd been thinking about him lately, but in abstract; she'd never expected him to turn up on her doorstep.

She had to get rid of him.

Right now. Before disaster struck.

"Look, I'm sorry, but I have no clue what you want after all this time."

He gave a casual shrug. "Just to talk."

"What can we possibly have to talk about?" Actually a whole load of stuff, but she needed preparation for that, a clear head, advice from a lawyer, and maybe a couple of hundred years to think about it. "I can't. I really can't. I have to leave for work. Right now."

When he just stood there, staring down at her, she gritted her teeth and resisted the urge to push him off the doorstep.

His eyes narrowed. Then he pulled a card from his back pocket and handed it to her. She took it automatically, her eyes straying to the road, expecting to see the car pull up any moment.

"Call me," he said. "Or come by the club. When this has sunk in, I would like to…talk to you."

When she didn't answer, his nostrils flared and something flashed in his eyes. "You remember the club? The place where you picked me up and fucked my brains out."

He turned and strolled away, hands shoved in his pockets.

"Ouch." The tension oozed out of her, and she leaned against the doorway, closed her eyes, and released a ragged breath.

When she opened them, he was gone.

By the following afternoon, Logan still hadn't gotten over his feeling of… What? Maybe that was the problem. He had no clue how he felt. The meeting certainly hadn't gone as he'd imagined, but then again, what had he expected? He realized, obviously too late, that he hadn't given any thought to his fantasy girl's feelings in all this. Hey, she was his fantasy girl. She was supposed to act in an appropriate fantasy-like manner.

She wasn't supposed to look at him as though he was all her nightmares rolled up into one big pile of dog crap that she couldn't wait to scrape off her sensible shoes. And that was only after she'd finally recognized him—which had taken far longer than it should have done considering they'd had hot, mind-blowing sex every night for a year.

In his dreams.

He'd spent last night lying awake, going over the meeting, trying to decide what his next move should be, if any. But Josh and Vito would have a field day if he gave in this easily. And he was one hundred and ten percent convinced she wouldn't be calling, or turning up at the club, any time soon.

She was nothing like he remembered, and certainly nothing like the sort of woman to indulge in his kinkier fantasies, which was a pity and a dash to his hopes. For a moment, he'd thought he'd gotten the wrong Abigail Parker. Josh's security company had found her for him. Logan had only had the name Abigail and her date of birth—she'd told him she'd been celebrating her eighteenth birthday that night—but Josh had said that was enough. Logan had asked for a name and address. Perhaps he should have asked for more. But when he'd examined her closely, the basics were all there. The dark mahogany hair, though it was caught up tight in some sort of bun thing, and the big blue eyes. Her mouth…

But he somehow remembered her as bigger. She was medium height, about five-five in her low heels, and she had a trim figure in a gray skirt that reached past her knees and a white shirt, buttoned up tight. Prim and proper. Especially when she'd pursed her lips and looked him over as if trying to work out what a tattooed, ex-con like him was doing on her pristine doorstep.

At first he'd been amused when she so obviously had no clue who he was. Then he'd been pissed off. Once she had finally recognized him, she had gotten rid of him so fast it should have been funny.

Except he wasn't laughing.

People had always looked at him and made assumptions about the sort of man he was—most of them bad and many of them correct—and it had never bothered him before.

And it shouldn't bother him now. So why the hell—

"Are we boring you, boss?"

The question dragged him from his thoughts, and he frowned. He realized he'd been staring at the toes of his boots where they rested on the chair opposite, when he should have been watching the woman on the stage. But it had taken him all of about five seconds to decide she wasn't suitable. They were a classy nightclub not a seedy strip joint. The dancers were there to provide a little glamour not a service for the customers.

He glanced at Jerry, his artistic manager, who sat beside him, in a crisp business suit. "No, not bored, just a little preoccupied." With Ms. Prim and Proper.

Still the question made him think. This had once been one of his favorite jobs—interviewing dancers for the clubs. Christ, what man wouldn't enjoy the show?

He studied the woman gyrating on the stage. She had impossibly red hair and impossibly huge tits only marginally covered by a sequined bikini top. Classy she was not. Nor was she prim and proper. She saw she had his attention and increased her efforts, gyrating to the low throb of the music. Reaching behind her, she tugged at the ties of her bikini top. Normally, at this stage he'd stop her and point out the whole classy nightclub thing, but he was worried.

What the hell was wrong with him?

Shouldn't he be feeling something right now? Something other than pissed off at a woman he hadn't seen in eleven years, and who wasn't even here, and probably never would be.

The dancer was doing this clever move, which made her nipples sort of rotate. Very impressive. But somehow he wasn't impressed. He looked down and contemplated the bulge in his jeans—not even a twitch. Once he would have taken the dancer up on the very clear invitation in her big brown eyes, just because he could, and because he loved women, all sorts of women, the more variety the better. And they would have both had a good time. Women liked him.

But the thought made him want to yawn.

Shit, he was only thirty-two. Wasn't that too young for a midlife crisis?

He loved running the nightclubs and had been doing it for ten years, ever since he'd gotten out of prison. His father, Rory, had believed he needed to keep busy to stay out of trouble. Though it wasn't needed; Logan had already decided he was never getting into trouble again. No way. But he'd loved the nightclub business from the start—the challenge, always something different going on, and an inexhaustible supply of gorgeous women to fuck. When had that lost its appeal? He couldn't remember the last woman he'd—

"I take it this one is a no," Jerry said, interrupting his

thoughts. "Pity. I like her. Looks like a nice girl."

Logan snorted, watching as Jerry got to his feet and crossed the room. He spoke quietly with the woman, who flashed Logan a look of abject disappointment, as though he'd broken her heart or something. She picked up her top, clutching it to her bosom, and spoke again. Jerry flashed him a look of amusement but nodded and helped the woman down from the stage. She tottered over to Logan, hovered in front of him. Actually, she did look like a nice girl; there was a hint of sweetness beneath the heavy makeup.

Across the room, the door opened and a woman slipped inside. Logan glanced over and did a double take. Abigail Parker. He almost laughed out loud, and suddenly he had an urge to high five.

Not cool.

Still, he couldn't keep the grin from his face.

The nearly-naked dancer must have thought the smile was for her. She took a step closer. "I thought we might go for a drink," she said, halting in front of him.

"Sorry, sweetheart, no can do." She'd probably heard he was a sure thing. And maybe once he would have been.

He peered past her to make sure Abigail was still there. She stood inside the door, looking around as if unsure of her next move.

The dancer shuffled her feet. "I really need this job. I have a baby and a dog and…"

There was a hint of desperation in her voice and he glanced back at her. He hated that. He looked from her to Jerry, who shrugged. "Okay," Logan muttered. "Take her on. But a week's trial only."

"Oh, thank you." She leaned down, dropped the top and kissed him on the lips, squashing her breasts against him. Nope, still no reaction from his dick. He glanced over her shoulder to where Abigail stood. She'd finally spotted him, and an expression of… He couldn't really define it. Pained horror, maybe, was stamped on her face. She caught him watching her and the expression was wiped clean. Then her tongue came out, swiping across her lips in a nervous gesture, and he felt a definite twitch.

And there was that urge to high five again.

He'd almost forgotten the nearly-naked woman clinging to him, but was grateful when Jerry took pity on him and tugged her free. "Go get dressed and I'll go through the terms and conditions of the job."

She smiled and hurried away.

Jerry crossed the room and flicked on the main lights. In the sudden brightness, Logan got his first good look at Abigail, a complete contrast from the dancer.

While she held herself with a certain confidence, as though used to difficult situations, there was an uneasiness in her face, a little line between her eyes. But she was here. That was all that mattered. Logan relaxed in his seat, put his feet back on the chair opposite, took a sip of scotch, and studied her some more.

"You want me to deal with her?" Jerry nodded in Abigail's direction.

"No, you go sort out our new dancer." He gave Jerry a sharp look. "Did you tell her to try the 'I'm desperate' and the puppy dog look?"

"I might have mentioned you're a sucker for a sob story. But don't worry. I'll make sure she fits in."

Logan shook his head. But Jerry was good at his job, so he put it from his mind and turned his attention back to more important matters.

When Abigail saw he was alone, she straightened her shoulders and headed his way. Logan took another sip of scotch and watched her lazily. She looked out of place. If he wasn't mistaken, she was wearing the same gray skirt from yesterday, topped with a black sweater this time. Her dark hair was pulled into the same bun thing at the back of her head, showing off the perfect heart-shaped face, large blue eyes, and wide mouth he remembered. He had a sudden image of her on her knees in that immaculate outfit, her mouth wrapped around his dick, and he shifted in his seat.

Yes, everything was definitely in working order.

She came to a standstill in front of him, her gaze sliding over him, lingering on the tattoos that snaked down his arm, revealed by the short-sleeved T-shirt. Something flickered in her eyes. No doubt she was confirming her judgments of yesterday. But it didn't matter, she was here.

Her gaze darted away then back, and she blinked a couple of times, shook her head, swallowed… He almost grinned and was about to put her out of her misery and offer her a drink, tell her he was really pleased to see her, when she spoke. "Mr. McCabe?"

Her voice was soft and low and sent a shiver down his spine that settled in his balls, flooding his groin with heat. And this time he did grin. The day was looking up.

"Call me Logan." He allowed his gaze to wander over her slowly, taking in the thrust of her breasts beneath the black sweater. They were full above a slender waist and rounded hips. And he was betting they were real. They'd feel soft in his hands.

And his dick jerked again. He put his feet on the floor and shifted his chair so she wouldn't see the reaction—he wasn't a complete boor.

Her eyes narrowed. Up close, they were as beautiful as he remembered, a mixture of blue and turquoise like the Caribbean Sea.

She cleared her throat. "Can we talk?"

We can do a hell of a lot more than that. But he kept those words to himself. He didn't want to scare her off. "We can do anything you like, sweetheart."

She frowned at the endearment. Her lips tightened and her fingers gripped the handle of her extremely large handbag. "I need to speak to you about something. Something important."

"You didn't seem to want to speak to me yesterday."

"You took me by surprise. That was all. It was…nice to see you. After so long." She took a deep breath. "So can we talk?"

To be honest, he couldn't think of anything they had to say to each other. But he was intrigued. More than that, he was hot and hard. And only a few minutes ago, he'd been worried his libido was dead. "Go on."

Her eyes darted around the room, coming back to him. "Could we go somewhere a little more private?"

That worked for him. They needed privacy for what he had in mind.

Maybe she was having the same idea.

Though if she was, she was hiding it well. He suspected that was wishful thinking on his part.

But perhaps she couldn't help but imagine what they'd be like together again. He was more than willing to comply. He pushed back his chair and rose to his feet. She took a step back, then pulled herself up straight.

"We can go…" He allowed his gaze to wander over her figure, because he wanted to look at her, and because he also wanted to piss her off, a little payback for yesterday. "…talk in my office."

Her eyes narrowed but she managed to force a smile. "Thank you."

Chapter Two

Oh God, could this get any harder?

He was being a total prick. But could she blame him after the way she'd behaved yesterday?

She'd been wallowing in self-doubt from the moment she'd caught sight of him smothered beneath a pair of the biggest fake breasts she had ever come across, and not doing much fighting, either.

The father of her daughter.

She'd almost turned right around and walked out. She tried to tell herself that you shouldn't judge a book by its cover. But if you did, Logan McCabe had a title something along the lines of *Fifty Shades of Hot*. He was sex on legs. Long legs, lovingly encased in faded denim that hugged his thighs and emphasized the bulge at his groin, which she was sure was getting bigger. She tried to keep her gaze away, but it kept flicking back all on its own. She was certain she must be bright red, with steam coming out of her ears.

And she was also pretty sure he was perfectly aware of the effect he had on her. His silver eyes gleamed with amusement, but at the same time his face held a hint of menace—she was guessing he hadn't been impressed by her reaction yesterday. Whatever the reason, the combination was terrifyingly intoxicating.

She was finding it hard to believe they'd had sex together. More than once. They hadn't been able to get enough of each other. Her body melted at the memory. She had to get a grip before she turned into a messy puddle on the floor. Maybe her reaction was just her body remembering—how had he put it so eloquently—that she'd fucked his brains out on that long ago night.

The annoying thing was, he was so not her type. She didn't go for bad boys. She liked nice, smart men in suits and ties. Men who were courteous and polite, and who didn't look her over as though mentally stripping the clothes from her body.

She followed him across the huge room toward a door in the far wall and tried not to stare at his ass. Though maybe, while there was no one around to see, she should look her fill and get over it. Somehow he'd transformed her back into her eighteen-year-old self. These days, she had a super-responsible job, was famous for nothing fazing her, yet here she was positively drooling over the most unsuitable man she'd ever encountered. Just because he'd been the first man to give her an orgasm. The only man to give her multiple orgasms. Her sex flooded at the memory. God, why did she have to remember that? Even at twenty-one he'd known his way around a woman's body, had pleasured her with his mouth, his hands, his huge… He'd been sensational, seeming to get off on her pleasure.

What had he learned in the long years since?

Stop thinking about sex.

This wasn't about her. It was about Jennifer. Had she made a huge mistake coming here? But really she'd had no excuse. Her last chance to back out had vanished when she'd done a quick background check on him this morning and discovered he had been in no further trouble, was in fact an upstanding member of the community—even if he didn't look it.

Her only hope now was that he wasn't the sort of man who would be interested in a ten-year-old daughter. With a bit of luck, he'd listen to her and tell her to go to hell.

Except that still left the question unanswered—why had he come to see her yesterday? She'd racked her brains and come up blank.

In front of her he moved with the lithe grace of a predator, a smooth glide. Under the bright lights his hair gleamed almost blue-black. Her gaze snagged on the black and red tattoos snaking around his arms as far as his wrist and others peeked out from the neckline of his T-shirt. He hadn't had that many tattoos eleven years ago.

He pushed open a door and stepped inside. Abby hesitated and then followed, finally turning to face him. He stood, hands shoved in his pockets, the look of amusement back in his eyes.

She hated that she was so transparent.

She took a quick look around the room. It was an office, with a big mahogany desk and a long black leather sofa. And suddenly it came to her. This was where Logan had brought her all those years ago. She'd had sex on that sofa. More than once. Oh God, why couldn't he have taken her somewhere else? It had been his father's office back then—a fact indelibly imprinted on her mind, as it was his father who had caught them the following morning, fast asleep and naked. If she remembered rightly, his father had been amused. She'd thought she might spontaneously combust.

"I'm glad you came." Logan dragged her back to the present. "I hoped you would—once you got over the shock. It must have been a surprise, me turning up on your doorstep after all these years."

Yes, it had definitely been a surprise.

Time to move this along. She'd get her bit out before she lost her nerve, then if he was still talking to her, she'd ask him why he had come to see her. "Mr. McCabe—"

"Logan," he interrupted.

She licked her lips. "Logan." What the hell was she supposed to say? She'd rehearsed this conversation so many times and now her mind was complete and utter mush. "I'm Abigail—Abby."

His lips quirked. "I'm quite aware of that…Abby."

She wiped her clammy hands down the sides of her skirt, exhaled loudly, and opened her mouth to tell him. Then lost her nerve. "Why did you come to see me?" Not what she was supposed to say.

Coward.

He took a step toward her and studied her, his head cocked. Then another step and another. As he circled her, she could sense his gaze playing over her body. Finally, he came to a halt in front of her. Reaching out, he pried her handbag from her fingers and dropped it on the sofa. She had to hold herself very still as his fingers stroked beneath her chin, before gently urging her head up so he could stare into her eyes. His were silver, and this close she could see the ring of black around the iris…so familiar. "I wanted to see you again."

"After more than ten years?" She shook her head, pulling free. He didn't try to hold her, and she took a step back. Obviously, she was being super slow witted. "Why now?"

He grinned, looking younger. The hint of menace vanished, and some of the tension eased from the room. "You could say I had an epiphany."

"You did?"

"A near death experience. I realized I wanted to see you again."

He still wasn't making any sense. "We had one night

together—"

"One pretty hot night."

"Maybe, but all the same, why would you want to see me again? And why now?"

He looked her up and down as if deciding what to say next. "You were my fantasy girl."

"Your *what*?" *His fantasy girl?* That sounded unlikely. She wasn't the fantasy girl type, and he must have had thousands of women since. If the one he'd just been groping was anything to go by, Abby was hardly his usual choice.

That fact didn't seem to be stopping him now. He trailed his knuckles down the skin of her throat, and a shiver ran through her. "You probably don't know it, but I had a little misfortune shortly after our night together."

Punching a cop was hardly a little misfortune, and she knew all about it. She'd gone to see him three months after their night together. This was the only place she knew to look for him. They'd told her he was in prison—for grievous bodily harm to a police officer. She'd walked away and tried not to think about him ever again, which had been a little difficult, considering the circumstances.

"Anyway," he continued, "I was inside for a year. And every night I dreamed about you. And me. Together." He must have seen something in her face because he grinned again. "Yeah, baby, we got to know each other pretty well in that year."

Ugh. He'd been jerking off to her memory. While he was in prison.

She should be horrified, but hell, she'd done the same. For weeks after that night, she'd dreamed of him, thought about coming back, offering herself for a replay. Right up until she'd realized she was pregnant, when the dreams had stopped and the nightmares began. It had literally torn her family apart, though in hindsight she knew that wasn't such a bad thing.

"So," he murmured, and somehow he'd gotten a whole lot closer. "I was in this accident a few weeks ago, and… you know, the whole life-flashing-before-your-eyes thing. Afterward, I got to thinking that maybe it was time I re-made the acquaintance of my fantasy girl. See what she was like in reality."

At a guess: nothing like he remembered. That night had been time out. She hadn't even been wearing her own clothes.

His hand still rested against her throat, and now it slipped around the back of her neck, burrowed into her hair and tilted her face up to his.

Move.

She needed to back off, tell him what she had come to say. She was betting that particular outcome hadn't played any part in his fantasies. But he was going to kiss her—the intention was clear in his eyes—and somehow, there was absolutely nothing she could do to stop it. She was petrified in to position, every muscle locked up tight.

No. No. No.

She was stronger than this. Wasn't she? But the words remained lodged in her throat.

"Do you know how many nights I dreamed of you and woke up so fucking hot and hard, and you weren't there? The things I dreamed about doing to you—nothing too kinky, honest. I'm a simple guy. Okay, maybe some of it was a little kinky." He grinned, swiped his tongue across his lower lip, caught it between his white teeth. "And now, here you are. I'm guessing I shocked you yesterday, but maybe later…maybe you were a little bit curious about what it would be like."

It?

Abby opened her mouth to explain why she was really here, but he placed a finger over her lips, stopping the words. "We can talk later."

Maybe he had a subconscious inkling that he wasn't going

to like what she said. All the same she had to put a stop to this now. She suspected, though she couldn't quite get her head around it, that Logan was about to attempt to re-enact some of those fantasies. And that *so* could not happen. Fantasies were just that. They had no place in the real world. Not his and not hers.

"I—"

He took a step closer, cutting off her words, so close the heat of his body radiated through the layers of her clothes, and the musky, male scent of him filled her nostrils. He was lowering his head. He was going to kiss her. This wasn't happening. Oh God, why had she never considered this happening? She took a step back, and he followed her. Another, and the backs of her knees banged into the edge of the sofa.

His other hand came up so he was cupping her face between his palms. She couldn't quite define his expression, but it made something warm and needy uncoil inside her.

He was going to kiss her, and she couldn't let that happen, couldn't let him believe she was available to fulfill some decade-old fantasy. The only way this would work was if they could be cool and detached about it.

He was coming closer, lowering his head, his gorgeous lips parting…

Stop right there.

She pulled away, ducked sideways, and put the sofa between them.

His eyes narrowed, but he still had that glint in his eyes. He was confident of her; she could see it in the lazy amusement in his expression.

She licked her lips and swallowed. "We need to talk."

"We will. Later. Right now we need to have a little trip down memory lane. Don't tell me you don't want to, Abby. Don't tell me that you aren't hot and wet for me under that prim little outfit."

She gritted her teeth. "I am so not…"

He raised an eyebrow and glanced down. She followed the direction of his gaze; her nipples were hard little peaks, clearly visible through her bra and sweater.

Traitorous nipples.

They ached to be touched. It had been a long time that was all. Too long. She'd had boyfriends in the past, but the last few years had been hectic, juggling her little girl and her job, so she'd pushed that part of her life aside to think about later and never gotten around to it.

He moved slowly, as though not quite sure of her, despite his words, as though she might run. And she thought about it, really she did, but she wasn't confident her legs would carry her. She gripped the back of the sofa to steady herself.

She didn't want this. Did she?

Maybe just once.

But sex would complicate matters.

Jennifer. Think of Jennifer.

She swallowed but didn't move as he came up behind her.

"This was one of my earlier fantasies." He leaned in close, whispering the words in her ear, sending frissons shivering across her skin. "So, you're the governor's secretary."

"I am?"

"A cliché I know, but I didn't have a lot to work with. Apparently, when you found out I was in prison, you were inconsolable—"

"I was?"

He kissed the side of her neck, and prickles ran down her spine. "Devastated. So you got a job at the prison to be close to me. Anyway, the governor has been called away, and we're alone at last. You want me…" His arm slid around her waist, one hand splaying across her belly, and he pulled her back against the heat of his body. Oh God. He was already rock hard, and his erection pushed against her ass, and her insides turned hot and molten. He was so big, and heat flooded her core, soaking her panties. "And, baby, you can have me, but we have to be quick, because he might come back at any moment." His tongue licked the side of her neck, and fire burned down through her body to settle between her thighs.

He nipped her earlobe between sharp teeth, and somehow her ass moved of its own accord—*traitorous ass*—pushing back against his erection, and he made a low growling sound deep in his throat. His other hand came around her, palming her breast, rubbing at the engorged nipple, sending darts of pleasure to her sex.

"Christ, I love your tits. There's no time to undress, but other times I'd suck them, lick them, rub my dick between them, until I came all over you. And afterwards, we'd do it all over again." He pinched the nipple and she gasped, biting her lower lip to try to maintain some last, small vestige of control. She stared down at that tattooed arm, the big hand, long fingers squeezing her breast, and the air was sucked from her lungs, leaving her breathless.

The hand on her stomach slipped beneath her sweater, pushing inside the waistband of her skirt. The caress of his rough palm against her bare skin did weird things to her insides. She pressed back against him, feeling him all the way along her spine, her ass, her head against his shoulder. His hand shifted lower and the button popped off her skirt, allowing him access.

"Sorry." He didn't sound sorry. "I need to see if you're as turned on by this as I am. Are you turned on, Abby?"

She would have liked to say no, but at that moment his fingers slipped inside her panties. There was no hesitation as he burrowed between her thighs. "Oh yeah," he murmured into her ear, his voice laced with satisfaction. Then his fingers slid between the folds of her sex.

Oh God.

"Holy shit, you are so wet." He rubbed one finger over her, and her knees buckled. The arm around her held her up, and she heard his soft chuckle in her ear. "You like that?" He didn't seem to expect an answer which was just as well. He slid his hand further into her panties, his finger finding the opening to her body and shoving inside, hard, so she gasped. "Your pussy feels like I imagined, hot and wet, and tight. It's going to feel so good wrapped around my dick. You want my dick in your tight little pussy, Abby? First though, I need you to come for me. In my fantasies you always came for me, over and over again, screaming my name. You going to scream my name?"

God, she couldn't even remember his name, couldn't remember *her* name, or why she was here, or why she shouldn't be doing this...

He pushed two fingers inside, stroking her inner walls, but that wasn't where she needed him. Her clit throbbed, so swollen and sensitive that if he would touch her there she knew she would—

He swiped the pad of his thumb lightly over her and she let out a little squeak. Withdrawing his fingers from inside her, he circled the swollen nub until she almost screamed with need, teasing her, while he sucked and kissed her neck. Her hips were rotating in little circles, right up until the point he flicked a finger over her, and she went instantly still.

"You like?" he murmured.

She shook her head, unable to answer, but this went way beyond liking. He chuckled against her skin as though he understood what she was thinking, then his fingers moved, pushing inside her again while he massaged the little nub with the heel of his hand. She clamped her eyes shut tight, as the pleasure coiled up tighter and tighter inside her until she thought she couldn't take any more. He pressed harder and finally she snapped, shattered, breaking her into a million pieces, lights flashing behind her closed eyes.

She was hardly aware as he pulled his hand free, stepped back from her, gripped the hem of her skirt and tugged it up over her hips. A hand in the small of her back pressed her down across the back of the sofa, as a thigh pushed between hers, spreading her legs. Fingers gripped in the top of her panties and she knew any second he'd rip them from her and she'd be exposed, ready, desperate…

He went still. "Fuck."

"What…?"

A knock sounded on the door, directly in front of her. The handle turned as Logan grabbed her shoulders, stood her up, and pushed down her skirt. She reached out resting her hands on the back of the sofa, took a deep breath.

"Looks like the governor's back, sweetheart." Logan's tone held a wry amusement. "Why the fuck didn't I lock that door?"

Her legs were shaking and little tremors of residual pleasure raced through her body.

A man appeared in the open doorway. Déjà vu. Tall and handsome, he was an older version of Logan, minus the tattoos: Rory McCabe, Logan's father, and the same man who had caught them last time.

Could this get any worse?

"Am I interrupting something?" Rory asked.

"Yes," Logan snapped.

"No," she said at the same time. No way could she go through with this now. She'd have to go away, build up her defenses, arrange to see Logan in a public place, and then she'd tell him about Jennifer. But right now she was so out of here.

"Sorry," she mumbled, "but I'm late for work. I have to go, I…" She clamped her lips closed. There was nothing else to say. She shuffled around the sofa, giving Logan a wide berth, grabbed her handbag from where he'd dropped it, and headed to the door—fast. Rory McCabe stepped aside for her. Nearly out, but as she went through the door, she couldn't resist one quick peek back. Logan was watching her, hands shoved in his pockets, a thoughtful expression on his face.

She really didn't want to know what he was thinking. Instead she made a dash for freedom.

Chapter Three

Logan stayed behind the sofa, where the fact that he was about to burst out of his jeans would perhaps go unnoticed. She'd come looking for him. He'd really thought she'd never turn up here. A grin tugged at his lips.

Rory closed the door and turned to face him, brows drawing together. "You look pleased with yourself."

Logan probably looked like a grinning idiot. So, maybe she wasn't the wild woman he remembered, but she'd felt good in his arms, hot and wet and so sweet.

"Who was that?" Rory asked. "She looked vaguely familiar."

That was interesting. Somehow he doubted Rory would remember her from eleven years ago, which meant he had seen her someplace since. Had she come looking for him before this, and maybe chickened out or simply not found him? "An echo from the past."

"And what did your echo want?"

Logan ran a hand through his hair. He'd presumed she'd had a rethink after he'd left yesterday. Decided she wanted to see him again. Now in hindsight, he wasn't so certain. She'd said she needed to talk to him, but he hadn't exactly given her a chance. Just jumped on her. But Christ, how many long nights had she kept him company, how many times had he jerked himself off to her image in his head. He knew it was partly because she'd been the last woman he'd slept with before his life had turned to complete and utter shit, but it was also more than that. They'd shared something pretty special and he'd meant to track her down and do it all over again. *How*, he didn't know, as she'd only told him her first name, but he would have found her somehow. Except he'd never gotten the chance. "I don't know what she wants."

Except she'd wanted him.

Against her better judgment he was guessing. He was coming down from the shock of seeing her and his curiosity was rising. Shit, his fantasy girl. "Something," he said. Hopefully helping him relive a few of his fantasies. If Rory hadn't turned up he'd be deep inside her right now. That thought wasn't helping his hard-on go away. "But we didn't get around to discussing it."

Rory sat himself down on the sofa and rested his head back, while Logan poured them both a scotch. He handed one to his dad, took the seat behind the desk, and sipped his own drink.

"Where the hell have I seen her before?" Rory muttered, eyes narrowed in concentration.

Rory knew a lot of people, many of them seriously dodgy. Logan hoped that wasn't the case with Abby, as he'd sworn off dodgy years ago. No way was he ever getting involved in anything related to his father's old life.

Rory McCabe was now totally legitimate, but that hadn't always been the case. The family business had been started up by Rory's father and built on illegal gambling, drugs, and prostitution. Rory had decided to go straight after marrying his second wife, Judith, a rich American socialite who had refused to have anything to do with him unless he turned his life around. Declan, Logan's half brother, had been groomed to take over and show a respectable front to the world. Logan hadn't resented his getting the position—Declan did it so well. Logan was never going to convince anyone he was respectable and he had no intention of ever trying. He knew what people saw when they looked at him.

He was a product of Rory's first marriage to an exotic dancer who he'd knocked up. They'd married because of Logan but couldn't stand each other and had quickly separated. Logan had lived with his mother until he was ten, used as a bargaining chip to get money out of his father. Finally, Rory had gotten so pissed off he'd made her a one-off offer she couldn't refuse and he'd gone to live with him. He occasionally saw his mother. Made sure she was okay. She wasn't all bad. She'd just hated Rory more than she loved him. He could sort of understand that, but the whole experience had left him with a less than rosy view of marriage.

He'd called his father Rory, not Dad, right from the start. But he liked him. They were similar and got on well together. He'd welcomed Logan into the family, and he'd never felt like an outsider. But no one had ever tried to make him perfect like Declan. By then it had been way too late anyway.

He knew Rory felt guilty about his time in prison. Rory had never done time, though not for want of trying on the law's part. All through Logan's childhood, they'd harassed the family, looking for anything they could use against Rory. Well, they'd never gotten anything on him; he was too canny. Unlike Logan, who'd been a total hotheaded asshole and deserved everything he got, if only for his stupidity.

He didn't blame anyone but himself.

Rory had written the nightclubs over to him when he'd gotten out, and he'd immersed himself in making them successful. He wasn't a businessman like his brother, or rather like Declan had been. Mr. Perfect Businessman had recently had a midlife crisis, and about time. He was now off exploring the world on a Harley with the love of his goddamn life. It made Logan grin every time he thought about it. He didn't believe in happy ever afters, but if anyone could make it, Declan and Jess would.

"Does she have a name?" Rory asked.

"Abigail Parker."

Rory shook his head. "No. Rings no bells. Fuck, where have I seen her before?"

Logan wasn't worried; he had a hunch she'd be back, and if she wasn't, he knew where to find her. He had to go out of town today—he had a meeting in Glasgow about a club he was on the point of purchasing—but as soon as he got back, he was paying her a visit.

"It will come to me," Rory said.

"You're losing it, old man. Senile decay."

Rory grinned. "Fuck you. You wait. I have a memory for faces and this will come back to me."

"Well, let me know when it does."

He had plans for Abby Parker.

Life was good and about to get a whole lot better.

He flew back to London the following afternoon. He wanted to check in at the club and after that, he was falling into bed. The night before, the new manager of his new club in Glasgow had taken him on a tour of the nightlife so he could take a look at the competition. He hadn't gotten back to his hotel until the early hours, and he'd been too keyed up to sleep.

Unfortunately, his plans were put on hold. His father met him as he walked through the main room to his office.

"Come on," Rory said. "I want to show you something. We'll take your car."

Rory refused to say anything else—he could be fucking annoying that way—but he had a sort of self-satisfied smirk on his face as he gave directions through the city.

"What the hell?" Logan said as they finally parked outside New Scotland Yard, the home of the metropolitan police— not his favorite people, and the last thing he needed right now. He had bad memories of this place. They'd brought him here after his initial arrest, when he'd known he'd fucked up bad.

No, he didn't need this. What he needed was sleep, followed by a visit to his fantasy girl.

"Come on," Rory said.

Logan sighed but followed his father around the front of the building and through the main entrance into a large reception area with a desk at one end. A group of people stood in front of the desk, but Rory made no effort to approach, just stood to the side of the doors they'd just entered. Logan still had no clue what the hell was going on.

"I told you I'd remember where I'd seen her."

Was he referring to Abby? Had she been arrested for something? "What the hell are you talking about?"

The group parted, and he caught sight of the uniformed officer behind the desk.

At that moment the officer—a sergeant, by the stripes on her sleeve—raised her head and stared straight back at him. Her blue-green eyes widened, and his only consolation was that she looked as shocked as he felt.

"You are fucking kidding me," Logan muttered.

Rory shook his head. "I wish I was."

"Let's get the hell out of here."

From the look of horror on his face, you would have thought he'd just discovered she was a serial killer. Across the room he stared back at her, accusation in his silver eyes, and maybe something else. Disappointment?

Must be a shock to find his prison fantasy girl was a cop.

She felt a twinge of guilt followed by disbelief at her reaction—she had nothing to be ashamed of. It wasn't as though he wouldn't have found out anyway. It was hardly a dirty little secret. She was proud of what she was. She couldn't remember ever wanting to be anything else.

The sad thing was, he hardly looked out of place in a police station—but on the wrong side of the law. Dressed in black leather trousers, black boots, and a black shirt, sleeves rolled up, open at the neck, showing the edges of his tattoos, he radiated bad-boy menace.

From the look on his face, she wasn't sure she'd get another chance to talk to him. He'd probably have the bouncers turn her away.

His hands were fisted at his side, and right then and there, she had a flashback to the feel of those hands on her body. She could hardly believe he'd had them down her panties within five minutes of them meeting. She'd been doing her best not to think about it. And failing—it had felt so good. How long was it since she'd come like that, even on her own.

If they hadn't been interrupted, she wouldn't have stopped him. After the first touch of his fingers on her sex, the thought of saying no hadn't even popped into her head. She'd wanted him inside her.

With one last disbelieving shake of his head, Logan whirled around and disappeared out the front door. Her gaze switched to the other man. She'd hardly noticed him with Logan there, but now she recognized Rory McCabe. She waited for him to follow his son, but instead he strolled across the space between them. Wiping her hands down the sides of her dark uniform pants, she straightened her shoulders. She hadn't done anything wrong. And it was none of this man's business even if she had. He looked like an older version of Logan, though his hair was short and flecked with silver. He had laughter lines on his face, but just then his gray eyes were icy cold.

"Police Sergeant Parker, I presume."

She nodded. "Mr. McCabe."

His gaze ran down over her uniform, and if anything his eyes got colder. "I don't know what you want with Logan, but stay the hell away."

She opened her mouth to answer, but he'd already turned around and was walking away.

A shiver ran through her. She'd met many people who, for whatever reasons, disliked or distrusted the police, and disliked her, but the hatred in Rory McCabe's expression shook her.

She was pretty much out of it for the rest of her shift. She was going to have to face Logan again. She'd made the decision, and the fact that he obviously despised her profession shouldn't change that. This was about what was right for Jennifer. It should make no difference if he hated her. It might even make things easier.

"Have you heard a word that I've said," Jack asked, making her jump.

Detective Sergeant Jack White had been a friend since they'd both joined the force on the same day, and they'd shared their goals of becoming detectives. Jack had moved through the ranks faster than her—he'd made detective three years ago, but she'd put her ambitions on hold until Jennifer was older and would maybe understand why her mother wasn't always there for her. But she'd recently taken her detective exams, passed with flying colors, and she was ready to apply for her dream job. As soon as a vacancy came up, she was going for it.

Recently Jack had made it clear he was hankering after more than just friendship, and she'd already decided that she was going to take him up on the offer. They got on well, and he also got on with Jennifer. He was a good man. And good-looking, too—tall, with sandy blond hair and a lean body he took good care of. Maybe he didn't make her go wobbly at the knees, but that had to be a good thing. Right?

"Sorry," she said. "I was miles away. It's been a long day." Fortunately her shift was nearly over.

"You want to go for a drink?" Jack asked.

"I can't, Jack. I'm exhausted."

"Okay. But soon?"

That was one of the reasons she liked him. He was so easygoing. Plus he understood the stresses of the job. "I'd like that."

She'd just spoken to her mother. Jennifer was already in bed. Abby was going to go home, have a long hot bath, go to bed herself, and tomorrow she would wake up ready to try again.

I can do this.

Everything would work out.

Once her replacement arrived, she signed off and went to the locker room and changed into street clothes, black pants and a white shirt. She checked her hair and makeup out of habit and headed out onto the street. Jack was leaving at the same time and he held the door for her—he was such a gentleman. "I'll walk you to the Tube," he said. She came into work on public transport; it wasn't worth the hassle of trying to drive in the city. Jack did the same, but he lived on the opposite side of London.

Once outside, she didn't get very far, her feet coming to a halt without any instruction from her brain.

Logan McCabe lounged against the wall outside the

building, arms crossed over his chest, exuding bad-boy menace. His gaze flicked from her to Jack, and his eyes iced over.

She glanced across at Jack. His brows were drawn together as he studied the other man. He was a detective; he had a sense about the bad guys. Obviously he didn't like the look of Logan. Logan's mouth twitched as though he found the other man's reaction amusing. But then, he seemed to find a lot of totally unfunny things amusing.

He unfolded his arms and pushed himself away from the wall then strolled the last few steps to come to a halt in front of her. "Abby."

"What do you want?" She knew she sounded belligerent, but she was super-aware of Jack listening to every word.

Logan raised an eyebrow. "You said you needed to talk to me." He shrugged one shoulder. "Here I am."

She wasn't ready for this, was still in turmoil from seeing him earlier, seeing his expression of utter dislike. That had gone, smoothed away, or maybe he was hiding it beneath the expression of vague geniality that didn't really go with the black leather and tattoos. Her gaze drifted down over his long, lean body. The shirt was tight across his broad shoulders, hanging loose over the black leather pants. She shifted her focus lower, to the pants molded to his hips and thighs —

"Abby?" Jack spoke from beside her and she jumped. She needed to keep her wits about her. Her eyes flashed to Logan's face. He was smirking as though he'd noticed her checking him out. Really though, how could he miss it. She cleared her throat. "It's okay, Jack. I do need to talk to Mr. McCabe."

"You want me to stick around?"

"No, I can handle this."

"She's very good at handling me. Aren't you, Abigail?"

Jack's gaze sharpened and Abby sighed. Logan was being

a prick. Again. "I'll be fine, Jack. I'll see you tomorrow. Mr. McCabe is an…old friend."

Jack gave a curt nod, and she watched as he walked away, then turned her attention back to Logan.

"Mr. McCabe? Very formal. I take it your friend there doesn't know I had my hand down your pants yesterday." He leaned in closer so his breath feathered her skin. "That you were hot and wet for me, and I made you come."

Low blow.

She swallowed. "Strangely enough, no I didn't mention that to him," she said. "What do you want?" She wasn't buying into the talking thing; she was guessing he had something else on his mind.

"Ask me nicely and I might tell you."

She shot him a dirty look but didn't even attempt to "ask him nicely."

He shrugged then raked his gaze over her body, taking in her clothes or, most likely, her lack of uniform. "You've finished for the day?"

She nodded.

"I'll give you a lift." He glanced around at their surroundings. "This place gives me the creeps."

She didn't want to go with him. She wasn't ready for the confrontation right now. Tired from the long shift, she wanted to go home. But Logan didn't wait for an answer, just jerked his head in the direction of the car park at the back of the building. For a second she contemplated making a mad dash in the opposite direction, but that would be pathetic, so she hitched her handbag onto her shoulder and followed him. His ass in black leather was as impressive as it had been in faded denim, but really she shouldn't be thinking like this. She was sure Jack had a great ass as well. Funny that she'd never really noticed it in the ten years since they'd met. She made a mental note to check it out next time she saw him.

Logan stopped beside a sleek black Ferrari. Wow. It suited him perfectly—long and lean and dark and no doubt a very fast mover. He opened the door, and she took a deep breath and climbed in. Inside it smelled of expensive leather and spicy cologne and a musky, male scent she knew was all Logan McCabe. Just the smell of him sent tingles to her belly. She was better than this.

He got in beside her, and suddenly all the oxygen seemed to be sucked out of the car and she couldn't breathe. She swallowed, forced air into her lungs, and concentrated on slow, steady breaths. She waited for him to ask where she was going, but he started the car without speaking. The engine positively purred as he drove out of the car park and into traffic. It was slowing down now, after nine, and most people in this part of the city were already home. He drove fast but within the limit. She had no clue where they were going, but couldn't bring herself to break the silence. Finally, he spoke.

"So you're a cop, Sergeant Parker."

"Yes." She didn't elaborate; she didn't have to justify what she was to him.

She'd been on the force for nearly ten years, had learned how to deal with the most difficult of characters and keep her cool. How did this man get to her? Could it be because none of those others had had their hands in her panties? None of them had made her come. Oh God, would she ever forget the feel of those long fingers, pushing inside her. She eyed up his hands resting lightly on the steering wheel. They were beautiful hands, with olive skin and long fingers, short nails. The tail end of a tattoo trailed over the back of one, but she couldn't make out what it was.

"You're very quiet. I thought you'd be interrogating me by now."

"Interrogating you about what?"

He shrugged. "Tell me one thing. Are you trying to set

me up?"

She'd been gazing out of the window at the passing buildings, now she swung her head around to face him. "Of course not. Anyway, you came to see me first."

"Yes. So I did. I have no clue why, but I actually believe you. So…?"

"So?"

"Yesterday, you said we needed to talk."

They did, but right now she didn't think she could make much sense. Would he hate her after she told him? Part of her knew she should have made more of an effort to tell him back when she had first found out she was pregnant. But he had been in prison. How could she? And maybe he'd want nothing to do with them. They'd had unprotected sex that night, which was majorly stupid, but she'd been drunk for the first time in her life, and he'd been the most exciting thing she had ever seen. She'd totally lost her head. But perhaps he'd made a habit of it and had left a trail of illegitimate children all across London.

"I have to admit, cop or not, I like the way you…talk." Logan interrupted her less than happy thoughts. "Yesterday I liked it very much. Until we were interrupted. So I thought we could go somewhere where we could 'talk' without the risk of being disturbed."

"Where are we going?" She glanced out of the window; they'd been driving along the embankment, the lights glinting on the dark water of the Thames, but now they turned off and headed north.

"My place."

That was a bad idea. A really bad idea. "I don't think so. I thought you were taking me home."

"Sorry, I have to go feed my dog." She eyed him suspiciously, and he cast her an innocent look. "What? You don't believe a man like me would have a dog?"

She didn't know what to believe. But she was suddenly intensely curious to see where he lived, to know more about this man. Because she knew so very little, and inadvertently he'd played a huge part in her life. Would maybe play an even bigger part in the years to come. She should know more about him. It was a responsibility. She'd done the basic amount of research on him, gone through the files to check that she wasn't introducing some hard-core criminal into Jenny's life. But he'd been clean since that one youthful indiscretion. In her experience people went two ways after a time in prison. Either they somehow turned themselves around, or they got worse. Logan must have made the decision to keep out of trouble, though he obviously came from a wealthy background, which would have helped. His father had owned the nightclub where they'd first met.

"How did you know where to find me?" she asked. She was pretty sure he hadn't known she was a police officer yesterday.

"My father. He was convinced he'd seen you around somewhere—he has an extremely suspicious nature. He asked around, and in the end one of the bouncers said he recognized you from a recent brush with the law. Apparently you took down his particulars."

"Nice company you keep."

"Actually, he's an okay guy, just has a hot temper and a crap tolerance for alcohol."

They were driving through an upmarket residential area now, wide streets with Georgian houses set back from the road by large gardens. They were close to Hampstead Heath, one of her favorite parts of London. It wasn't the sort of area she would have expected him to live—though again, what did she really know of him?

He turned off the road and pulled up in front of a set of metal gates. After he pressed a button on the dashboard, they opened and he drove through, along a curved drive that led to the front of a beautiful Georgian mansion. She knew a little about property prices around here, and this had to be worth millions.

"You live here?"

"Yeah. I moved here a few months ago. I lived in an apartment before that, in the city center, but then I sort of inherited the dog and…" He shrugged. "This place backs onto the Heath. It's perfect."

He'd moved house for a dog?

He climbed out while she was still trying to process the information, and came around and opened the door. She scrambled out, suddenly off balance.

The house was big, with a wide staircase leading up to a dark red front door, seeming more a family home than somewhere a bachelor would live.

"You're not married are you?"

"Christ, no."

His answer was emphatic. Obviously, not a big fan of marriage then.

What a surprise.

She stood for a moment staring up at the building, wondering what the hell she was doing here. Had she been totally deluded? She'd thought that she could keep her emotional distance, tell him about Jennifer, and allow him limited, controlled access if he wanted it. And it would all be smooth and painless. She'd always liked everything nice and clean cut, organized. As a child she'd striven to be the perfect daughter, then the perfect mother. She worked hard to be the best she could at her job. Now she had a weird sensation that she was about to screw up majorly. For one thing, she was getting the inkling that Logan wasn't going to be controlled about anything.

She cast him a quick glance. He was standing by the front

door, looking down at her. She couldn't read his face; he was amazingly good at hiding his expression, though as she stared, something hot and dark gleamed in his silver eyes. He pushed open the front door and stretched out a hand toward her. "Welcome to my humble abode."

Hmm, there was absolutely nothing humble about Logan, including his abode. But she forced herself to step forward, jumping as the front door clicked shut behind her. She was in a wide hallway, decorated in cream and dark red. It felt like a home. A number of doors led off from the central area and a staircase led up to the upper floor. The floors were wood and everything gleamed. She became aware of a scrabbling noise as Logan headed toward the door opposite. "Stand back," he muttered and opened the door.

A huge dog hurtled out, sliding on the shiny wood floor. An unrecognizable breed, maybe some Great Dane, Alsatian, a few other things. He hurled himself on Logan, who rubbed his head, then the dog turned and raced toward Abby. She held her ground and he skidded to a halt, thrust his head against her groin, and snuffled.

Abby crouched down, pushed him away slightly, and stroked his massive head. "He's lovely."

"He's a total monster. My brother took him in as a stray then decided he wanted to go traveling."

"So you took him."

"He's a guard dog."

Someone who liked dogs couldn't be all bad. "Of course he is."

"You like dogs?"

"Yes. I was never allowed one as a child—my father hated the mess."

"Grunt," he called to the dog, who whined and nudged Abby in the stomach. "He's not very well trained. Grunt, come!"

The dog reluctantly turned and loped off, following Logan. She stepped closer and watched as Logan opened a door to the back garden and the dog bounded out. Logan closed the door and turned back to her. For a minute he studied her, head cocked on one side, a question in his eyes.

"What?" she asked.

Chapter Four

She sounded vaguely belligerent, as though she was gearing herself up for a fight. Pity. He had no plans to fight her. He hadn't meant to go back to the police station. He'd been shocked and pretty much horrified when he'd found out what exactly she did for a living. He'd grown up distrusting the police, and things had only gotten worse when they'd locked him up on a rap most people would have walked away from.

But that didn't change the fact that he wanted her, and he wasn't used to not going after what he wanted. He was ninety-nine percent sure she wasn't setting him up, though he had no clue what she thought they needed to talk about. She'd managed not to talk to him quite happily for eleven years. Unless she had some fantasies of her own, and his visit had stirred them up. He liked that idea, and he was willing to play along. He'd even chat with her afterward.

But not right now. Right now, he had no plans to chat. On the drive over he'd been tossing around a few of his more repetitive fantasies, deciding which to…tackle first, and he'd gotten hot and uncomfortably hard.

Christ, even in that uniform she'd turned him on. Now that was a surprise.

Him fancying a copper—it was beyond inconceivable. "It's funny," he said, "I can usually spot the police a mile away, but you…"

"Me what?" The belligerence was still there.

"Well, let's just say I would never have guessed it. And I'm willing to overlook that little character flaw. Are you hungry?"

She shook her head. Good. Neither was he. "Come through."

He led her from the kitchen into the large sitting area. Through the French windows, he could see Grunt as he raced around the garden sniffing everything. Logan pressed a button on the wall, and curtains slid across to cover the glass. He didn't want Grunt trying to get in on the action. Abby halted in the doorway, looking warily into the room as though it were some sort of den of inequity.

She really wasn't his type; he liked his women a little on the uncontrolled side. Abby Parker was neat, her clothes conservative, not a hair out of place. Though that wasn't how he remembered her that night. And he'd spent enough time going over it in his mind. She'd been wild, which made this Abby an enigma, and a challenge. He liked challenges.

Could he make her lose control?

"Come in," he said. "I'll get us both a drink. Scotch okay?" She'd drunk tequila that night, though she didn't look much like the tequila type anymore. He spent a lot of time at the club guessing what people drank. He usually got it right. Miss Priss over there probably drank lemonade.

He didn't wait for her to answer, just poured them both a scotch and waved her to the sofa. She took the chair instead, back straight, knees together. She accepted the glass but put it down on the table beside her without taking a sip.

She cleared her throat.

He was wavering between scenarios with her on top, with her breasts in his face, or a blow job, though on top might be easier to negotiate. Or on her back on the dining table, or bent over the sofa… Maybe he'd save that for later.

She was obviously considering what to say, how to start, but he really didn't think he'd have too much trouble persuading her to his alternate plan. Yesterday she had melted for him. Within minutes she'd been hot and wet. His dick twitched, and his balls ached. Time to move this along. Before she got around to saying whatever it was she was working herself up to, because while he couldn't begin to guess what she wanted, his intuition told him it wasn't going to be anything good.

She licked her lips, and his dick jerked again. His pants were uncomfortably tight but hopefully he'd be out of them soon. He almost didn't want to start. He'd been fantasizing about this for so long. What if it was a disappointment? What if he couldn't make her come? In his fantasies, she'd come for him hard and frequently, usually screaming his name.

Fuck. What if she did say no? He swallowed his scotch in one go and put the glass down next to hers. Then he strolled around the back of her chair, stepped up close.

She was staring fixedly ahead. "So," she began. "I—"

"Shush," he murmured.

"No really, I've got to—"

"We'll talk later. I promise." Much later. Maybe even weeks later. Or months. He had three hundred and sixty five days' worth of fantasies to work through, and he was sure there were some he'd like to do more than once.

Reaching across, he pulled the pins from her hair. She didn't move. After yesterday, likely she knew what to expect when he got her alone. If she hadn't wanted this, she wouldn't have come. Her hair was dark, glossy brown with glints of ruby, and he ran his hands through the silky soft strands. Loose, it reached past her shoulders. As he massaged her scalp, she groaned and leaned into the movement.

He trailed his fingers down the side of her neck, felt her shiver, then slipped them inside the open neck of her prim shirt, played along the sharp jut of her collarbone, and lower to cup one full breast in his palm. She went even more still, holding her breath, but when she didn't protest, he squeezed gently.

Part of him couldn't believe she was here, and he was here, doing this, when he'd dreamed about it for so long.

But one thing was sure. He needed to get inside her, and soon, or he was going to spontaneously combust. And it would be messy. He withdrew his fingers from her shirt and strode around to face her, holding out his hand. She peered at it for a second, like he was some sort of devil trying to lead her astray. Then, as though she couldn't help herself, she reached out slowly and slipped her fingers into his.

The tension oozed from him, and he realized he hadn't been totally sure of her. And if she'd said no there was nothing he could do. He didn't know how to seduce a woman. Normally they seduced him, and he'd grown lazy.

Studying her through half-closed eyes, he allowed the hunger to build inside him. Her cheeks were flushed and her lips slightly parted. He stroked a finger across her plump lower lip, and her tongue flicked out. At the feel of her tentative touch, fires roared in his belly, sizzling along his nerves and sinking to his groin. He was in serious danger of losing it. That had never happened in his fantasies, but his cock was throbbing with the need to be inside her.

"Do you remember that night?" he asked.

She shook her head.

"Liar." Slipping a finger into the neckline of her shirt, he flicked open the first button, and the next, and the next. Her eyes widened, but she said nothing as he tugged the material off her shoulders and tossed it to the floor, leaving her in a white cotton bra. He was going to buy her some new underwear; he had a hankering to see her pale skin against black lace. Her breasts were fuller than he remembered—he could live with that. He stroked the pad of his thumb over her nipple and she moaned. With one hand he circled behind her, undid the catch on her bra, and peeled the soft cotton from her skin, taking a step back so he could look his fill. Her breasts were full, but firm, topped with dark red nipples, already swollen. He lowered his head kissed one, then sucked the other into his mouth, caressing the taut nub with his tongue as she almost fell against him.

She appeared dazed, as though her responses came as a surprise, and it occurred to him that maybe it had been a while for her. No worry. She'd be so turned on by the time he got to that point that he'd slide inside like he belonged there.

Right now, he needed her totally naked. He kissed her nipple one last time, straightened, unfastened her skirt, and pushed it down over her hips, hooking his fingers in her panties and tights on the way. And there she was. Naked and all for him. In the flesh. Real. To do with as he pleased.

"Holy shit."

He swallowed as the last of his blood supply drained into his cock. But for a minute he couldn't move, all he could do was stare. She was different, but the same. She'd been slightly more slender, now her breasts and hips were fuller, though her waist was possibly smaller, so she curved beautifully. Her skin was pale, the curls at the base of her belly glossy brown like her hair.

He raised a finger and motioned for her to twirl. Her eyes narrowed slightly, but she slowly turned. His breath caught in his throat, and his mouth went dry. Her ass was smooth and rounded. He stroked a fingertip down the length of her spine until it hovered over the cleft between her buttocks. Leaning closer, he whispered in her ear. "Open your legs, sweetheart."

She shuffled her feet so he could stroke along the line of her ass cheeks, sliding between her thighs to push one finger between the plump, hot folds of her sex. She was soaking wet, and he sank to his knees and burrowed his nose between her legs, breathing in the scent of hot, aroused woman. His fantasy girl wanted him. That was the biggest turn on of all, and he knew then which particular fantasy he was going to go for first. With a last kiss on her left buttock, he got to his feet and took her hand, tugging her gently.

She resisted a little. "What…?"

"Let me do this, okay. Go with me. I had a lot of time to think about how to please you. You'll like it. I promise." She caught her lower lip between her teeth, but gave a quick nod.

"So, fantasy number two. We're back in the governor's office. He had this big leather chair…" With a finger between her breasts, he pushed her gently into the big leather chair she'd been sitting in earlier. She pulled her knees up to her chest, looping her arms around her legs, and stared up at him, her eyes huge.

"Sorry, sweetheart, but that's not going to work."

He peeled her hands free, and without giving her a chance to protest, he wrapped his fingers around her ankles, straightened her legs, and pulled them apart. "Fuck, but that's pretty." Her thighs were slender but lightly muscled, and her sex glistened. His dick throbbed to remind him he needed to move this on, or embarrass himself. He rested one of her ankles over the arm of the chair, then the next, so she was wide open to him.

Resting his hands on the soft skin of her knees, he leaned in close. "So, Sergeant Parker," he murmured. "I bet you're used to being in charge. You want to tell me what to do."

She blinked up at him.

He smiled. "Don't want to talk anymore?"

She shook her head, and he sank to his knees in front of her. She was the sexiest thing he had ever seen, in dreams or reality, sprawled in front of him, open to his gaze. He swiped his tongue over his lower lip, and her breath hitched in her throat. He wanted to take his time, but there was something he needed to do. He flicked open the fastener of his trousers, and groaned as he lowered the zipper and his cock sprang free, rock hard and ready. But he'd waited this long, he could wait a while longer. This was going to be perfect. For both of them.

He slipped his palms under her ass, used his thumbs to part her sex and stared for long seconds. She was his dream and she was real.

"Logan, please."

His gaze shifted to her face. "Tell me what you want."

"Touch me."

"I am touching you."

"You know what I mean."

"Ask me."

"Kiss me."

He smiled. "Where?" He dropped a kiss on the soft skin of her inner thigh, and she groaned. "There?"

She shook her head.

He could see her clit pouting from her sex, already swollen, dark red. Breathing in deeply, he filled his nostrils with the intoxicating scent then dropped a slow kiss on the tiny nub. Her muscles locked up tight. He wanted to take his time, but he had a hunch she would last all of about ten seconds. She was desperate, and that intrigued him. He left the sensitive spot and licked along the length of her sex, pushing his tongue inside, tasting the spicy sweetness of her, licking at the moisture, circling her clit but never quite touching until her hips were lifting, pushing against his mouth. He held her steady, his fingers digging into the soft flesh of her ass, lapping at her, fighting down the need rising in him.

And he was burning up with need.

Finally, he moved back to her clit, flicked it with the tip of his tongue, drew it gently into his mouth, and suckled. Her hands clutched his hair, her hips circled, and he sucked harder, felt the moment she came apart for him. He drew back, studied her pretty sex, her pussy pulsating. As the tremors eased, he massaged her clit with the pad of his thumb and she came again, her head falling back, her pulse frantic under the pale skin of her throat.

The wait was over.

He drew a condom out of his back pocket, tore it with his teeth, and rolled it down over his erection. Then he dragged her to the edge of the chair and pushed slowly inside her. She was tight but so wet that he slid in with ease, groaning as her slick muscles squeezed around him. Lodged deep inside her, he took a moment to savor the feeling. Like coming home.

On to fantasy number three.

He gripped her ass and pushed to his feet, still deep inside. Turning, he sank onto the chair, shifted her slightly so she was kneeling, legs on either side of his hips. He settled her as his cock pulsed, shifting his hands to her hips. Slowly, he lifted her then released her so she sank back onto him. *Heaven.* He raised her again, and she rested a hand on his shoulder, found a rhythm, rising and falling. He could feel her along the whole length of his cock, the pleasure tugging at his balls. As she took over, he rested his head back, watching the sway of her breasts. He slid one hand up the indentation of her waist, over her rib cage, to cup her breast, lifting it for the caress of his tongue.

So close.

As she sank down, she rotated her hips, massaging her clit against his pelvic bone with each stroke until she was squirming on top of him. She was going to come again; he could feel her tension building. He gripped her hips, pressing her down, rubbing her harder against him, and her head fell back as she screamed her release. The sensation of her pulsating around him was enough to tip him over the edge, and he pumped into her, the release going on and on as she rode him.

Finally, he slumped back into the chair and pulled her close.

He kissed her hair and closed his eyes. "You were supposed to scream my name, but otherwise that was perfect."

She'd forgotten everything, including his name.

Who he was, why she was here…

He was still fully dressed while she was totally, totally—it didn't get more bare-assed than this—naked. She was wrapped tight in his arms, and while she hated to admit it—because this was in no way part of the plan—it felt right. More right than anything she could remember, and for some reason that made her want to cry. And she never cried. As a child, she'd learned early on to keep everything locked in tight. Now here she was draped all over a badass bad boy, and she had the most almighty urge to bawl her eyes out. Maybe she should go ahead. It might frighten him off and that was a good thing, because however right this felt, it was wrong. She didn't fall into bed with strangers.

Except this one.

Twice now.

And both times it was out of this world, orgasmic.

At least he'd used a condom tonight. Obviously he'd gotten more responsible with age. Or maybe fed up with paying for unplanned offspring.

He was still deep inside her. She wriggled and a wave of

residual pleasure rippled through her. The zipper of his pants was chaffing against her inner thigh and she shifted a little. Time to make a move. Go back to real life and work out how to put things back on track. Again.

Was he asleep? She made to pull away, and his hands tightened on her hips, holding her in place.

"Don't move," he murmured without opening his eyes. "Not yet."

"Why? Won't the governor be back soon?"

He chuckled, but didn't release her, and she straightened her spine so she could look at him. His hair had come loose; she had a vague memory of digging her fingers into it while his mouth had been between her legs. Oh God, his mouth had felt so good. She'd never relaxed enough with any other man to allow him to do that, had always felt too self-conscious to enjoy the act. But she hadn't felt self-conscious with Logan; he'd driven everything but the feel of his lips and tongue from her mind. When he'd sucked her into his mouth, she'd exploded.

"Stop wriggling," he muttered.

She stopped. She didn't want to disturb him, she wanted to look at him some more. She might never get another chance. If she got the plan back on track, this wouldn't happen again. He was truly stunning—heavy-lidded eyes, with thick black lashes that lay across his high cheekbones, a straight nose, a long jaw, shadowed with stubble, and the most beautiful mouth she had ever seen, the upper lip curved, the lower full.

"You can kiss me if you want, sergeant."

"No, thank you."

"I can feel you staring."

His eyes flicked open, and he held her gaze as his hand slid up to curve under the hair at the back of her head. Slowly, he drew her down, his lips parting beneath hers, his tongue pushing inside. He kissed her for long minutes, deep wet kisses that she felt all the way down to her toes. He finally drew back, leaving her shaken to the core. How could a stranger make her feel so good? So right?

She needed to get out of there, but before she could do anything he wrapped his arms around her and got to his feet, cradling her against his chest. She was by no means small, but he carried her with ease, kicking the door open and heading up the wide staircase, into a bedroom and through to the huge bathroom beyond.

As he set her down on her feet, she opened her mouth to tell him she was leaving, but before she could get the words out he started unbuttoning his shirt. It occurred to her that he'd seen her naked. Wasn't turnabout fair? And she could revisit the whole now-or-never argument, because obviously she was never doing this again. So if she was going to see him naked—and she really wanted to—this was her only chance.

He shrugged out of the shirt, and she stared at his broad chest with the smooth swell of muscle. His skin was olive and perfect. The black ink of his tattoos snaked around from his back, curling over the lean ridges of muscle on his stomach. But it wasn't the tattoos that held her attention but rather the glint of silver at his nipple.

He glanced down and grinned. "I had a dare with my brother Declan. He's such an uptight bastard. He said he would if I would. So we did, and, shit, it hurt like hell."

Then his hands moved to his waist. He kicked off his boots and pushed the leather pants down over his lean hips, turned away to toss the condom into the bin before coming back to her.

He was already semi-hard, and as she stared, his shaft twitched and filled with blood, jerked to attention until it stood upright against his flat belly. Her mouth suddenly dry, she swallowed and licked her lips.

"I like the way you look at my cock," he said. "Like you're

hungry for it and you'll let me do whatever I like with it." His gaze slid over her. "You okay? I'm guessing it's been a long time for you."

Her eyes narrowed. "Why would you guess that?"

"Male intuition. Are you sore?"

She shook her head. It was a slight lie; there was an ache between her thighs, but there was also a tingling.

"Good."

He reached past her and turned on the water in the huge walk-in shower, then took her hand and sort of hustled her inside.

"Another fantasy?" she asked.

"No. Funnily enough, shower scenes didn't play a big part in my prison fantasies."

She didn't want to even think about why not.

"But," he continued, "this seems like the perfect excuse to get my hands all over you." He gave her another little push, and she was under the spray. She reached up and tied her hair into a knot, closed her eyes, and relaxed.

She'd failed totally. She hadn't told him about Jenny, and she hadn't kept her distance. What a major cock-up. In more ways than one. She was just frustrated, that was all. Her body had needed this. It wasn't as though she'd saved herself for him or anything. She'd had boyfriends, but the sex had never been particularly good. She found it hard to switch off, and it left her feeling a failure, and she hated that. In the end she'd given up. Her life was so busy, juggling Jenny with her career and lately studying for her detective exams. She'd hardly noticed the lack of men in her life. Or so she'd thought.

Why him?

She had no clue. He was the opposite of everything she needed, which was a father for Jennifer. Someone supportive of her career. Someone who wanted the same things out of life.

At that moment his hands cupped her breasts, squeezed, and her eyes flew open. "It looked like you were getting too serious there," he murmured.

She glanced down as his soap-slick hands glided over her breasts, her skin tingling beneath his touch. He stepped closer, into the warm spray of water, so the droplets beaded on his thick lashes. His slippery hands continued their slow exploration of her body, down her rib cage, between her thighs, and she gasped. He massaged her gently, then his hands slipped around to soap her bottom, squeezing her ass cheeks.

As she raised her head, he lowered his and they kissed as the warm water washed over them. He pressed along the whole length of her body, his erection hot and hard against her belly.

"I want you again," he muttered.

Well, she wasn't arguing.

He sighed against her mouth, before drawing back. "No condom."

"Oh."

He reached behind her, turned off the water, and grabbed a towel. After drying her quickly, he rubbed the towel over his head. His long hair was damp and he pushed it off his face, grasped her hand, and tugged her out of the shower, through the open door and into his bedroom. It was a huge room dominated by a massive bed with a crimson cover.

He looked from the bed, to her, and back again.

"Hands and knees."

"What?"

"I'm going to fuck you from behind. You okay with that, sergeant?"

Her sex was tingling, heat pooling at her core. Her body obviously liked the idea. She crawled onto the bed, and for a second wondered where her body-consciousness had gone. She'd never before felt entirely comfortable naked. Now here she was crawling onto the bed, ass in the air, for a man she'd only ever actually met four times in her entire life.

"Further," he ordered from behind her, and she crawled another foot onto the bed.

"Shit, that is pretty. Open your legs."

She parted her thighs. Raised her ass a little bit higher.

"Jesus, I can see you all wet for me."

She heard the rustle as he tore open a condom packet, and held herself very still, waiting for the first touch.

His hand came down on her ass in a resounding slap and she yelped, turning her head to glare over her shoulder at him. "Hey, don't do that."

"You don't like? In this particular fantasy, you liked it a lot. Sure you don't want to try? Just a nice gentle pat."

Did she? This was definitely the last time she was going to get naked with Logan. Maybe she owed it to herself to try everything. Just once. "Okay, but not hard. Anyway, I thought you said you weren't into kink."

He grinned. "Sweetheart, this is not kink. This is playing. Kinky would be if I was doing this dressed from head to toe in black latex and wielding a paddle."

She giggled. "Or a riding crop."

"You know your bottom does amazing things when you laugh. But this isn't supposed to be funny. Now hold still."

She held her breath, but when the next tap came it was gentle and felt unbelievably good, so her ass lifted all on its own. He slapped her one more time and then one hand rested on her hip, holding her steady as he pushed inside. He was big and hard and filled her completely.

How had she lived without this?

Chapter Five

Logan sat up abruptly. The room was dark but he could tell he was alone, the bed empty beside him. But the warm musky scent of sex lingered, and reaching out, he found the sheets still warm.

By the time they'd finished, he'd been barely able to move, so sated he didn't want to even try. He'd brought her again and again until finally releasing his own control and coming in a huge swell of pleasure that had crashed over him, leaving him limp and useless. Then he'd thrown the sheet over them, dragged her close, and listened as her breathing evened out. She'd been asleep in minutes.

He'd lain awake a while longer trying to get his head around it. His fantasy girl, here in his bed. And she'd been every bit as good as he remembered. Better.

Except for the policewoman part.

That definitely hadn't been part of his fantasies.

He ran a hand through his hair. Where the hell had she gone? She wouldn't sneak out on him, would she? There was no sound from the bathroom.

He flicked on the bedside lamp. Yup, she was gone. Then a door banged downstairs. Pushing off the sheet, he got to his feet, found a pair of jeans, and pulled them on.

He had an idea she was running. And for some reason, he didn't want her to make a clean getaway. Funny, he usually made sure he went to the woman's place so he could be the one to make a speedy escape when he was ready—usually about five minutes after the sex was finished. It was weird—and not particularly pleasant—to be on the other side.

He went quietly down the staircase. A light peeped out from under the living room door and he pushed it open. She stood with her back to him, fully clothed, so she hadn't planned on coming back to bed.

He felt a little…used.

He cleared his throat, and she jumped and whirled around, huge handbag clutched in one hand, cell phone in the other.

"Where are you sneaking off to?"

She stared at him, her gaze fixed on his naked chest. He liked the way she looked at him. So did his dick, coming to sudden life. Somehow he didn't think she was going to stick around for another of his fantasies. Pity.

"Home," she said. "I have an early shift."

"Wait. I'll drive you."

"There's no need. I called a cab. It will be here any second."

He studied her for a moment. For a woman who'd just experienced multiple orgasms, she didn't appear very relaxed. "Are you running away, sergeant?"

"There's nothing to run away from. We had a good time, but it won't happen again. We have nothing in common." She hesitated, nibbled on her lower lip, and gave a small shrug. "As you pointed out, I'm a police officer and…"

"…and I'm an ex-con?"

She shrugged again. "More along the lines of you've made

it very clear you hate cops. I'm a cop."

"Maybe I'm willing to make an exception. Anyway, I don't have to like you. I'm not looking for long-term or happy ever after. I don't believe in that crap. And you don't have to like me. All we have to do is accept that for some reason we have fucking awesome sex together. You remember that bit, sergeant? You remember the bit where you came all over my face?"

She pursed her lips and sniffed. "Well, maybe I need more out of a relationship." Her eyes widened and she backtracked quickly. "Not that we have a relationship or anything."

He chuckled. "You don't think I'm the sort of man to have relationships?"

"Honestly?" she asked, clearly making no attempt to keep the incredulity out of her tone. "When I saw you yesterday, you were half buried beneath the biggest pair of breasts I have ever seen."

His lips twitched. "I was interviewing dancers."

"Really?" She arched a brow, but was saved from saying anything more by the sound of a car horn from outside. Presumably her taxi. "I have to go."

For a second, he considered stopping her, arranging to see her again. But he had a hunch she wouldn't be too receptive to that idea. For now, he'd let it go. He knew where she lived and where she worked. He stepped aside as she approached the door and let her pass, though his fingers itched with the need to reach out.

He followed her into the hall. "I had a good time, sergeant," he said as she stepped through the front door and into the night. "Perhaps we can do it again sometime."

He thought she wasn't going to answer, then her muttered words floated back to him as she hurried down the gravel drive. "Not a chance in hell."

Abby managed two hours sleep. She thought about trying for another half, but she wanted breakfast with Jenny before she left for school.

Jenny was at the table along with Abby's mother when she dragged herself into the kitchen. As always, she looked at her daughter with awe, finding it hard to believe she had produced this exotic creature. Now, after seeing Logan again, it was clear exactly where Jenny got her looks—she was the image of her father, from her shoulder length glossy black hair to her silver eyes rimmed with black, her strong nose, and her wide mouth. Abby had never noticed the resemblance before. Or maybe it was truer to say she'd avoided the comparison, and it hadn't been hard as the years passed and there was nothing to remind her. Now it was like a slap in the face.

And Jenny was going to be tall. At ten she was already taller than most of her class, with a lanky frame she would eventually grow into. No, there was no doubt who her father was—she was a mini Logan minus the tattoos and, hopefully, the badass attitude.

"Morning," Abby mumbled and dropped into a chair.

Her mother shoved a mug of coffee in front of her, and she breathed in the scent.

"You got in late," her mum said. "I thought you finished at eleven."

"I had to see someone. We got to…talking and…" She shrugged. She couldn't exactly get into details, not with Jenny sitting opposite. Her mum gave her a weird look, maybe taking in the red rash of stubble burn along her collarbone and throat. She hugged her robe tighter around her. More stubble burn decorated her inner thighs—luckily her mum couldn't see *that*, or the faint bruises on her breasts. Logan hadn't been rough, but he hadn't been gentle either.

How had she matched up to his fantasies?

She rested her head on her hand and let the conversation wash over her; they were discussing some project Jenny was doing at school.

Finally, Jenny turned to her. "I'll be late home tonight." She got to her feet and picked up her school bag. "Sara's dad is taking us skating." She placed an inordinate emphasis on the word "dad," and Abby winced.

Jenny came around the table, gave her a peck on the cheek, though she suspected there was more to come.

"Maybe if my dad knew about me, he could take us skating one day," Jenny said.

A picture flashed in her mind, Logan shepherding an unruly bunch of ten-year-olds around the local roller-skating rink. Somehow the image wouldn't gel. Not for the first time, she wondered if she'd done the right thing going to the club, seeking him out. After the way he'd left the day he'd turned up on her doorstep, she was pretty sure Logan wouldn't have looked her up again, however powerful his epiphany.

"Maybe," she said.

Jenny beamed as though she'd gotten a result, then a car beeped outside and she ran out to meet her lift to school. A few of the local mothers took it in turns, though Abby's mother took hers, as it was hard to work around her shift times. She didn't know how she would have managed without her mum's help. For a time, when she'd first found out she was pregnant, it had looked like she would have to try. Her father had refused any help unless she had an abortion, and that had never been an option.

"Well, she's tenacious, if nothing else," her mum said. "So, are you going to tell her?"

"I think so."

So far she'd kept the information vague with Jenny. It had been easier when she was younger. She'd accepted anything

Abby told her, which was that she'd lost touch with her father, and he didn't know about her. It seemed for the best, open ended, so later she could tell her...something else. Maybe the truth. But over the last year, Jenny had become fixated on the idea of her father, wanting to know everything, and she was getting harder and harder to put off with vague responses. Abby had been torn between telling the truth and telling a downright lie. She hated lies, but she wanted to do what was best for her daughter, and maybe a man like Logan McCabe was a worse option than no father at all.

She'd still been undecided when he'd turned up on her doorstep. And she hadn't been totally convinced when she went to the club, or when she had climbed into his car last night. But deep down, she knew it was the right thing to do.

"Definitely," she said. "I'll go see him today." Somewhere public, or maybe she'd go to the nightclub during her lunch hour. Stay out of the back office.

"You want to talk about it?" her mother asked. "You never did tell us anything about him."

"I didn't know anything about him. He was a one-night stand. My only ever one-night stand," she added. This was her mother after all.

"And you never tried to tell him back then?"

"I did. When I found out, I went back to where I'd met him. I was going to tell him. He wasn't there. He was in prison."

"Oh."

"Exactly. I didn't try again. I thought that we'd be better off without a man like that in our lives. But Jenny wants to know him, and how can I keep it from her? One day she'll find out, and I'd rather it came from me."

"You've been in contact with him?"

Pretty much every part of him. Heat washed through her. "Yes, but I haven't told him yet. We got...sidetracked."

Her mother's eyes narrowed. "You saw him last night?"

She nodded.

Her mother gave her a long look. "Well, I hope you took precautions this time."

"Mum!"

"Don't 'Mum' me, Abigail Parker. You look well and truly shagged."

"Mum!" She was repeating herself but couldn't think of a lot else to say.

"And about time," her mum said. "I've been worried about you, with just Jenny and your job. A woman your age needs a man."

"I haven't got a man. It just… happened."

"Again. Just tell me one thing—that he won't hurt Jenny."

"I don't know." She chewed on her lower lip. "He's not a good man. But I don't think he's a bad man either. He'll maybe want nothing to do with her." She pressed a finger to her forehead. "We'll have to wait and see. But I plan to tell him today."

Really she did mean to tell him. But by eleven she still hadn't made the call. She realized she didn't actually have a number for him and was going to have to call the club and hope they would put her through.

"Are you okay?" Jack asked.

She glanced up from the desk where she was working on the shifts for next week, when she was off desk duty and back to heading the emergency call team. She was looking forward to it; she liked to be out on the streets.

"I'm fine. Just busy."

He perched himself on the edge of the desk. "So what did Logan McCabe want with you last night."

That got her attention. "You know him?"

"No, not personally. But I worked on the money laundering case Declan McCabe brought in last year."

"Money laundering?" She hadn't been involved with the case.

"Some cartel was using the family company to launder money. Declan McCabe stumbled across it and came to us. So I met the family. Declan was a good man, though he had no love of the police. Now, his father is a real piece of work—I got the impression he was pissed off at his son for involving us. He would rather have solved the problem himself."

Declan was the brother Logan had mentioned the previous evening, the one with the matching nipple ring.

"Could he do that?"

"Probably. He has the contacts. Rory McCabe's father came over in the forties, carved himself out a piece of the East End, and held on to it by sheer bloody-mindedness. They were into everything—drugs, illegal gambling, prostitution…"

"But not anymore?"

"No. Rory took over and for a few years he was the scourge of the East End, but something changed and he decided to go straight, clean up the company. Declan was groomed to take over, and as far as I know they're squeaky clean now."

"And Logan?"

"He wasn't involved with the case, though I met him once. He now manages the nightclubs. But he's been inside, Abby."

It pissed her off that Jack was telling her this, as though she wasn't capable of making her own judgments.

"I know. And don't worry—it was nothing important."

He looked as though he wanted to ask more, but he knew her well enough to recognize when to not push. "Well, keep away from him. He's trouble."

She didn't answer, but irritation flicked at her insides. Jack had admitted he didn't know Logan, so how could he know he was trouble? Of course, there was the little fact that he *looked* like trouble. Big trouble. But that was beside the point.

"So how about dinner tonight?" Jack asked.

A refusal hovered on her lips, but she swallowed it down. Maybe that's what she needed. A date with a nice guy, to put things in perspective. But she couldn't face it tonight. "Perhaps next week."

For a moment his eyes widened, no doubt because he'd gotten even that much of a positive response. He smiled. "I'll hold you to that."

When he'd finally gone back to work, Abby sat and stared at the phone for a full minute. Before she could seriously consider letting Jack into her life, she needed to clean it up a little. She picked up the phone and dialed the number of the club from memory. "Could I speak to Logan McCabe, please?"

Logan sat in the leather chair, his feet on the desk in front of him. He had paperwork to do—his least favorite job—but he hadn't been able to concentrate since Abby's phone call.

She wanted to talk to him

He wanted her to suck his cock.

Somehow he had to bring her around to his way of thinking.

He couldn't believe he wanted her again already. He hadn't been this randy since he was a teenager. But at the same time, he couldn't deny a hint of curiosity. What the hell did they have to talk about?

He really hoped it wasn't some sort of police business. That would totally piss him off. The clubs were clean. He was clean, and if she thought to try and prove anything else, she'd be sorry.

However much he wanted that blow job.

Finally, the phone rang. It was Mark on the door. "There's a copper here to see you."

So she'd turned up in uniform. He hoped that wasn't a bad sign. "I'll be right out."

He pushed himself up and headed for the main door. It was open, but Mark barred the way. Abby stood behind him, impatience stamped on her face. "I'm not here to arrest him, just let me in."

"We're closed."

"I'm not here to drink either. He's expecting me."

"Mark," he said and the bouncer turned around. "It's okay." He tipped his chin to indicate the other man should leave them, and waited until he'd disappeared into the club.

Abby huffed, obviously annoyed at being kept on the doorstep. She was in uniform, crisp and neat, her hair in that bun thing, not a strand out of place, her hat clasped in her hand, flat black shoes gleaming on her feet. She could be posing for a fucking recruitment poster, she was so goddamned perfect. He had an overwhelming urge to mess her up.

"Is this a business call?" he asked.

She glanced down at herself and shrugged. "No. It's my lunch break and I didn't have time to change. In fact I don't have much time at all so could we go inside. Please."

He studied her for a moment longer, to piss her off. Her lips were slightly swollen from his kisses, and he had a sudden image of her on her knees, mouth open, his dick at the ready. "Come in."

He stepped aside and gestured for her to enter, leading her through the huge, almost empty room. Some of the clubs opened during the day for lunch, but not this one. They were closed until eight that evening. A few people were around, cleaning, stocking up the bar, but the place was quiet.

He headed for his office opposite but halted when he realized she was no longer following him. He turned to find she'd stopped in the middle of the room.

Her glance flickered to the black door and back to him. "Could we stay out here? I really do need to talk to you."

"And you can't do that in my office? You think we might find something more interesting to do?"

She shuffled her feet. "Maybe."

At least she was honest and wasn't trying to deny the attraction between them. It occurred to him that maybe she thought the uniform might provide some sort of protection against him. He had told her that he hated coppers; perhaps she believed it would turn him off. In fact he found the whole idea of stripping her out of it a total turn on. And if he did persuade her into the blow job, she could keep the uniform on and put that sexy little hat on her head. He almost groaned at the image.

"Logan?"

It was the first time she'd called him by his name, and he liked it. Glancing around, he gestured to one of the booths situated on the edge of the room. He sat down, and she slid onto the leather seat opposite.

"You want a drink?" She looked like she needed a drink. Whatever it was she had to say, she wasn't happy about it, and his curiosity grew.

"No." Her tongue poked out, and she swiped her lower lip, leaving it glistening. He was pretty sure she wasn't aware of the effect it was having on him. "I'm on duty."

"How could I forget?"

She placed her hat on the table, straightened it, and rested her hands primly on her lap. For someone in a hurry she was sure taking her time about this.

"So," he prompted.

She licked her lips again. If she really wanted to talk, she should stop doing that.

Finally, she took a deep breath. "You have a daughter."

Chapter Six

For a second the words didn't make sense, and Logan presumed he must have misheard.

She cleared her throat. "Actually, *we* have a daughter. Her name is Jennifer, and she's ten and she would like to meet you."

He went still as he studied her across the table, trying to unravel the words. He had a ten-year-old daughter. Was she fucking kidding?

When he didn't speak, because he really couldn't think of anything to say that would make any sense, she continued, talking fast, "I know this must be a shock."

"You reckon?" He shook his head. "You expect me to believe that I have a ten-year-old daughter and all of a sudden you've decided I need to know. Excuse me if I'm a little skeptical."

A pulse beat under the white skin of her throat. She reached into her pocket and pulled out a photograph. She glanced at it and her expression softened briefly. Placing the picture on the table, she nudged it toward him with one finger.

He didn't want to look; he had no clue how he was going to deal with this. She had to be lying. But why? Had he set this charade in motion when he went to see her? Some sort of revenge plot? His brain was numb and in no shape to come up with a plausible answer. He caught her gaze as she nipped her lower lip between sharp white teeth. Finally, he forced himself to look down and stared.

The photo showed a head and shoulders shot of a young girl with dark hair and huge gray eyes. She was the spitting image of his half sister Tamara at that age. He was six years older than Tamara and could remember her well. "Jesus." He ran his hands through his hair. Other than that, he could think of nothing to say. He had no doubt that he was looking at his daughter. What he couldn't understand was why she was telling him this now? Why the hell had she never told him before?

He glanced up from the photo to glare at her, and she winced visibly. "I'll understand if you don't want anything to do with us," she said.

Some of the numbness wore off, replaced by an icy trickle of rage. "You'd like that, wouldn't you?"

"No, of course not." She licked her lips again, a telling gesture; she was nervous. Good. Though this time it did nothing to him at all.

"Why?" he asked.

"Why what?"

"Why tell me now?"

"I told you—Jenny wants to meet you."

Christ, his ten-year-old daughter, who he hadn't even known existed until seconds ago, wanted to meet him. How did he feel about that? Fucking furious. "I'm surprised you didn't tell her I was dead."

A flush washed over her face, and something flashed in her eyes.

"Christ, you thought about it didn't you?"

"I…" She took a deep breath. "Look, I can see you're angry—"

"Really. Why the fucking hell would I be angry? Maybe because you kept the fact that I had a daughter secret from me for ten years, and now you walk in here and expect me to take it calmly."

"I tried to tell you."

"Obviously not very fucking hard."

He saw the first flickers of anger in her eyes. "When I found out I was pregnant, I came here to see you. I didn't even know your full name, just this place. They told me you were in prison. That you'd been convicted for assaulting a police officer."

Of course. He'd been arrested the day after he'd first met her, had been denied bail, and sentenced to eighteen months. He'd gotten out on good behavior after twelve, but he would have been inside when she had the baby.

"I was eighteen," she continued, "My father is a lawyer, and I was supposed to be starting law school that autumn. So yes, visiting my baby's father in prison was a little outside my comfort zone."

"And after that?"

"It seemed easier to…ignore your existence. It never occurred to me that you'd want to know. We had a one-night stand. There was nothing between us."

"Except a baby."

She went silent, tracing an invisible pattern on the tabletop with her fingertip. Finally, she looked up. "I did what I thought was right for my daughter."

Yeah, because having a man like *him* for a father was obviously a shitload worse than no father at all. He couldn't believe the bitterness that washed over him at that thought. He was used to people taking a look at him and presuming he was a badass. It had never bothered him before. Hell, he'd taken a certain pride in it.

"So why didn't you tell her I was dead? That would have been nice and clean. No nasty, unsuitable ex-con of a father to explain away."

"I won't lie to you. I thought about it. I was still thinking about it when you came to see me." She rubbed at her forehead dislodging a strand of mahogany hair, ruining the perfect exterior. He had an urge to yank out the pins, mess her up further. "But it isn't fair on Jenny to lie. She has a right to know. And one day she'll find out. So I checked you out, and when I found out you hadn't been in any more trouble, I—"

"Decided to tell me the good news." Jesus, how much had she checked him out? He was a wealthy man. Was that what it was about—money? But he didn't think so, however angry he was. "What about me?" he asked. "Was it fucking fair on me? Did you ever think about that?"

Her eyes widened, no doubt at the anger in his voice. Then she slowly shook her head. "No. It was never about you. Always about Jenny. I don't know you...didn't know you. I had to think about what was best for her. And I have to tell you, if you'd been to prison again after that first time, I would not be here now."

Part of him could understand that, but most of him was seriously pissed off. What the hell right did she have to judge him? And find him wanting?

"I'm her mother. It's my job to protect her." She picked up her hat, and he realized that she was leaving. She'd dropped this bombshell and now she was going to calmly walk way.

"I have to get back to work," she said.

Maybe it was for the best. Maybe he needed some time to let this sink in, to think it through before he said anything else, because he suspected that right now he might say something he would ultimately regret.

"Call me when you decide what you want to do."

What the hell was there to decide? "I want to meet my daughter."

"Well, call me when you've calmed down, and we'll discuss it."

He gritted his teeth; he was goddamn calm.

"My number is on the back of the photo," she said and slid out from the booth. He sat back and watched her walk away, hat clutched in her hand. As she reached the door, Rory entered. He held the door for her and spoke softly. She snapped something back. Logan couldn't hear what she said, but whatever it was made his father raise his eyebrows.

Finally, the door closed behind her.

Logan sat back in his seat, his mind whirling. He wasn't quite sure if he'd imagined the encounter. Picking up the photo, he studied it some more. No, she was definitely real.

He glanced up to see Rory standing beside the booth.

"What did you say to her?" Logan said.

"I asked her what the fuck she was doing here."

Logan shook his head. "And she said?"

"She said 'go to hell.'" He grinned. "You know I might quite like her…if she weren't a cop. So what put her in such a pissy mood? And what *was* she doing here?"

Logan handed him the photograph. "It seems I have a daughter."

Rory studied the picture for a few seconds and whistled. "Holy shit." He shook his head. "You and the police sergeant?"

"Well, she wasn't a police sergeant back then." No, she'd been an eighteen-year-old girl. Could he really blame her for the choices she'd made? Hell, yeah, when those choices included cutting him out of his daughter's life. He could sort of understand why she had done it, but he wasn't ready to let go of his anger just yet.

He'd make a bloody good father. Wouldn't he? Truth was, he had no clue. He'd never even thought about a family. Never wanted one woman enough to settle down. He'd always presumed he would never marry. After all, he was hardly surrounded by role models.

But he'd grown up to the age of ten—the same age his daughter was now—barely knowing his father. Though he'd been aware of Rory's existence, his mother had made sure that they didn't spend time together. She'd even told him that Rory didn't want him, had never wanted him, which might well have been true at the time. All the same, Rory had made the most of a bad situation, and when Logan had finally gone to live with him, he'd never doubted that his father wanted him around.

What did his daughter think? That somewhere she had a father who didn't give a shit, who'd never wanted her. He'd make sure she knew different. He might make a crappy father, but his daughter would know it was Logan who was lacking. Never her.

"I need a drink." He stood up and crossed to the bar, pulled a bottle of single malt scotch and a couple of glasses from the shelf below, and carried them back to the booth. His father had taken a seat and was still studying the photo as Logan slid in opposite and poured them both a drink.

"I don't think there's any doubt she's a McCabe," Rory said.

"No. She looks like Tamara."

"She looks like you."

They sipped their drinks in silence for a minute. Logan emptied his glass then refilled both. He looked at Rory and something occurred to him. "You realize this makes you a grandfather."

Rory choked on his drink. "Bugger."

"Yeah."

"So what happens next?"

"I meet her." A cold, hard lump settled in his stomach. What if she took one look at him and ran for cover?

"Is her mother okay with that?"

"I presume so. Apparently she wants to meet me. That's the only reason Abby told me. Otherwise I would never have known."

"Is that all she wanted? Not money?"

"How the hell should I know? We haven't exactly gotten around to discussing details yet." His dad was a cynical bastard. Anyway, he supposed he should pay something toward her maintenance. How had Abby coped alone all these years? Had her family helped? He knew absolutely nothing about her, though she'd obviously managed to carve out a career for herself, which couldn't have been easy.

Shit, the mother of his daughter was a police woman. No wonder she was wary of letting him into their lives. He picked up the photo again and studied it. There was nothing of Abby; she was all McCabe. Had that pissed her off?

God, he had a daughter. It was beginning to sink in.

Would she like him? Or would she take one look at him and decide he should have stayed away. Maybe he should have a haircut or something. And he couldn't believe he was thinking like that.

"Her name is Jennifer," he said. "Jenny."

"Nice name."

He poured more scotch. It wasn't every day you found out you were a father. What if she hated him? "I'm scared."

"Daughters are scary things."

"Thanks, grandpa." He pushed himself to his feet.

"Where are you going?" Rory asked.

"To phone the mother of my daughter." At the last moment he grabbed the bottle of scotch and took it with him to his office.

"Well, tell her I take back what I said."

He stopped and stared down at Rory. "And what did you say?"

"That she should stay the fuck away from my son."

"A little late for that."

"Well, I wasn't in possession of all the facts."

"Neither was I."

Two days since she'd told him. It seemed like forever.

Abby couldn't say the reveal had gone badly, though it hadn't gone as she'd expected either.

If she was honest, she'd thought he wouldn't be interested. That he'd maybe accuse her of wanting his money or something, and she'd been all ready to throw that back in his face. She wanted nothing from him. They'd managed up until now and would manage in the future.

But he genuinely wanted to meet Jennifer, and if she wasn't mistaken, he fully intended to be part of her life.

How did she feel about that?

I don't know.

Her thoughts had taken on a surreal quality, her life spiraling out of control. Oh God, she hoped this was going to work and she wasn't making a mistake of gargantuan proportions.

"Are you okay?" her mum asked.

"Yes. No. I don't know. Ask me in a few hours' time." When this was all over. Logan was coming to Sunday lunch. She'd thought that their first meeting would be better for Jenny among her family and familiar surroundings.

"Is he really that bad?"

"No. Yes. I don't know."

Her mum laughed. "You know, I'm looking forward to

meeting him. The boy who sent my perfect little girl off the rails."

"He's hardly a boy. And I was never perfect."

"Yes, you were, but I understand why." She gave her a quick hug. "You were being what you thought we wanted you to be. And I'm really sorry we put those pressures on you."

"And I'm sorry I screwed up."

"You didn't. What happened was for the best, and I don't regret anything."

When her father had insisted Abby have an abortion and go on with her legal studies, her mother had finally, after years of toeing the line, stood her ground. She'd left Abby's father and stayed with her daughter. Abby would always feel guilty about that, but at the same time, her mother seemed happier now than she could ever remember her being during Abby's childhood. Her father had been a criminal lawyer from a good family who'd done the right thing and married his pregnant hairdresser girlfriend. But her mother, and later Abby, following her lead, always felt that they had to be on their best behavior. Always smart, always well-behaved...

"Anyway," her mum said. "There's something I wanted to tell you. I—"

She broke off as Jenny entered the room. Dressed in jeans and a pink shirt—she'd changed clothes about six times—her face was pale; she looked a little like Abby felt.

"What if he doesn't like me?" she asked.

"Of course he'll like you." She gave Jenny a quick hug. "Remember, he's probably as nervous as you. He's never had a daughter before. I bet he's changed his clothes about six times this morning as well."

Jenny giggled, then went serious. "I should be wearing a dress."

"No, the jeans are good."

"He'll think I'm a tomboy."

"You are a tomboy."

She wrinkled her nose. "Oh."

Another hug. "You'll be fine. Don't try to be something you're not just for someone else. People need to love you as you are."

"Amen to that," her mother said, and the words sounded heartfelt.

At that moment a loud rumble came from outside on the street, as some sort of vehicle pulled up, followed by silence as the engine was switched off. It sounded like a bike. He'd come on a motorcycle?

Her mum crossed the room and peered out through the window. "Holy crap," she muttered.

"Mum!"

"Sorry, but…"

Abby came up beside her and stared out through the glass. Logan sat astride a huge, gleaming black Harley. Jenny came to stand next to her, and Abby put an arm around her shoulders and hugged her close. As they watched, he pulled off his helmet. His black hair was tied back into a ponytail, revealing the sharp angles of his face. He wore black jeans and a black leather jacket. He didn't look like anyone's dad.

"Is *that* my dad?" Jenny asked in awed tones.

"Yes."

"Sara is going to be so jealous."

Abby caught her mother's gaze over Jenny's head, and her mum grinned.

Out on the street, Logan swung his leg over the gleaming machine with an almost animal-like grace. He stood for a moment studying the house, and she had the urge to step back out of sight. But there was no hiding today.

This was really happening.

"Are you sure *you* don't want to go change, Abby?" her mum asked. "Put on a pretty dress? Some makeup perhaps?"

She was wearing tailored black slacks and a white shirt. Boring, but somehow she didn't think Logan would be taking much notice of her today. This was about Jenny. She'd wanted to merge into the background.

"No thanks."

"At least take your hair down."

She frowned.

"Yes, mummy. Don't you want to look pretty for daddy?" Jenny reached up and tugged the clip from her hair so it tumbled over her shoulders.

"Hey."

The doorbell rang and she had no time to do anything about it. Taking a deep breath, she gave Jenny and her mum a quick smile and headed into the hallway. Then she took another deep breath and opened the front door.

As Logan walked up the drive, a prickle ran down his spine. He glanced to the side and saw the curtain twitch.

Was Abby watching him, regretting that he had ever come back into her life?

Was his daughter there?

Christ, get a grip.

He couldn't remember being this scared since his first night in prison. As he came to a halt at the front door, he closed his eyes for a moment, took a deep breath, then pressed the doorbell. It seemed like an age before he heard footsteps. The door opened and Abby stood there. He glanced behind her but she was alone in the hallway.

"Hi," he said, handing her the bottle of wine he carried and resisting the urge to wipe his palms down his pant legs.

I can do this.

"Come in." She moved aside so he could pass, closed the

door behind them, and followed him. "She's through there with my mum," she said waving a hand toward another door. "Did I mention my mum would be here? She lives with us. We would never have managed…" She was talking fast, and sounded as nervous as he was. That calmed him a little. As she leaned past him to open the door, he breathed in the scent of lemons, and the familiar smell dragged him back to the other night, the taste of her, the feel of her wrapped around him.

He slammed a lid on those memories. Now was not the time.

The door led into a lounge, but their surroundings faded as his gaze latched on to the girl standing in the center of the room, hands clasped in front of her, silver-gray eyes huge. He swallowed the lump in his throat and stepped through the door. There was no mistaking his daughter, and the knots in his stomach tightened as they stared at each other.

"Hello."

He almost jumped as a woman stepped forward, a pleasant smile on her face. She held out her hand. "I'm Rachel, Abby's mum." She didn't look old enough. While she had Abby's heart-shaped face and blue eyes, her hair was blonde and curly and hung to her shoulders.

He shook her hand. "I'm Logan."

Abby stepped up close to him. "And this young lady is Jenny."

He returned his attention to his daughter. She was so… big. He hadn't expected that. She was tall—almost as tall as Rachel—and slender. How could he have been instrumental in making something so beautiful? He was finding it hard to believe she was part of him. "Hi, Jenny."

"Hi…" Jenny trailed off.

He hadn't considered this—what did his daughter call him? Maybe he should have discussed it with Abby first. To hell with that. "Call me 'dad.' If you want."

Jenny gave a shy smile. "Hi, Dad."

His breath hitched, and for a moment he had no clue what to say or do... or even how to speak.

Rachel shook her head. "It's uncanny, the likeness between the two of you. Let me take your coat, Logan."

He shrugged out of the jacket and handed it to her. Beneath it, he wore a black button down shirt, the sleeves rolled up, and he caught Jenny staring at the black and red tattoos snaking down his arms. What would she think of him?

Rachel handed a glass of wine to Abby and an orange juice to Jenny. "Logan?"

"A beer would be great." He glanced at Abby. "Don't worry, sergeant, I'll just have the one. You won't have to arrest me today." Jenny giggled and he turned back to her. "Is she really strict with you as well?"

She nodded.

"Liar," Abby said. "I have to help your grandma finish cooking the lunch. Why don't you show Logan your room?"

For a few seconds nobody moved, and his brain froze. Then Jenny obviously took pity on him and slid her hand into his. Hers felt small and fragile, and the knot tightened in his gut.

"Come on," she said, leading him out of the room, only letting go of his hand as she headed up the stairs. He followed her, glancing back once. Abby stood in the doorway watching them, brows drawn together, nibbling her lower lip. Was she regretting this already?

Hard luck.

Jenny took him to a small room at the back of the house, decorated in shades of purple with posters of ponies on the wall. Maybe he could get her one for Christmas. Or maybe not. Rory had showered him with presents when he'd first gone to live with him; it hadn't made things easier.

Once on her own territory, Jenny started talking non-stop, pointing at things, explaining what they were. He lost track, just collapsed on the bed and listened to the sound of her voice. He guessed she was as terrified as he was. He wished there was some way to put her at ease, but he was new to this and had no clue. "Jenny," he said when she paused for a moment. "Are you okay with me being here?"

She peeked at him shyly and gave a quick nod.

"Good. You know," he continued, "I didn't know my dad until I was your age."

She'd been replacing a book on the shelf—her favorite apparently—and she turned to him, eyes wide. "You didn't?"

"He and my mum didn't get on. I'm just saying, I know how hard this is for you. But I want you to feel free to talk to me, to ask me anything."

She thought for a moment; he could almost see her mind working. "Do you and mum not get along? Is that why you haven't been around?"

He thought about his answer and blew out a breath. Honesty was a bitch. "No. That was my fault. I got in a…bit of trouble soon after we met, and we lost touch. Your mum and me—we don't really know each other."

"But you're going to?"

"Of course. And so are we. So…favorite food?"

She grinned "Pizza."

"Me, too. Hey, we must be related."

She giggled. At that moment, Abby called up the stairs that lunch was ready. This time Jenny's hand slid into his easily, and something melted deep inside him. He'd never been good at relationships, but somehow he had to make this work.

At the table, Abby seated him next to Jenny and opposite her mother.

Throughout lunch, Jenny kept up a constant buzz of conversation as though she couldn't switch off. Abby and Rachel added the odd comment when they could get a word in, but they didn't try and slow her; maybe they realized she needed to get it out of her system. Taking their lead, he ate his meal almost in silence. When he'd finished eating, he pushed his chair back and relaxed, watching her as she chatted. Finally, she ran out of breath.

"Why don't you come and help me get some more drinks, Jenny?" Rachel asked, rising to her feet. Jenny gave Logan a reluctant glance but followed her out of the room.

Logan shook his head. "Is she always this…intense?"

"No," Abby said. "She's normally a little more relaxed."

He gave her a wry smile "Me, too."

"You're doing great. She already likes you."

He blew out his breath and ran a hand through his hair. "She does?"

"I can tell."

He sagged in his chair as some of the tension drained from him. "I don't think I have ever been so shit-scared in my life. I wanted to bring her something, and then I remembered all the times I accused Rory of trying to buy me off."

"No, you did the right thing."

He glanced to the door where they could hear Jenny talking in the kitchen. "I'm surprised you're not in a constant state of exhaustion."

"She'll crash soon. She's running on nervous energy."

He gave her a long look, studying her face, seeing the lines of strain etched around her mouth. This meeting hadn't been easy for any of them. "Then maybe I should go. I've a lot to think about. But she's wonderful. You did a good job, and I know it can't have been easy."

She bit her lip and glanced away. "Thanks."

He stood up as the other two came back from the kitchen. Crossing the room to his daughter, he bent down and kissed her on the forehead. He thought quickly about what to say; he didn't want to pressure her but he needed to leave her in no doubt that he would see her again. "It's been lovely to meet you, Jenny. Maybe next time I can take you out somewhere."

Jenny beamed.

Hell, he'd got it right.

He shook hands with Rachel and turned to Abby. "Will you see me out?"

Something flickered in her eyes—maybe she didn't want to be alone with him—but she pushed back her chair and rose to her feet, leading him out into the hall. He pulled the door closed behind him and followed her to the front door.

"Wait a second," he said. He needed one more thing before he left.

She turned to face him, eyes widening when she found his so close. He glanced back at the closed door before taking the final step closer, which brought his lean length flush against her body. His hand came out and slid under the hair at the nape of her neck. He tugged her closer as his mouth came down, and he delivered a swift, hard kiss before pulling back.

His fear had drowned out his anger for a while. Now it came roaring back to life. "I can't believe I have a daughter. I can't believe she's ten years old and I know nothing about her." A tic twitched in his cheek, and he gritted his teeth to not say more. They had to work this out, and him blowing up would not help. All the same, he needed to make one thing perfectly clear. "I won't be kept out of her life."

She swallowed. "I won't try."

"Just as well. Because you'd fail." He gave a curt nod. "I'll be in touch."

Dizziness washed over her, and she forced herself to hold it together. It wouldn't do for him to see how much he affected her. But his words had shaken her to the core. She touched her lips as the door closed behind him. Her mouth tingled. If she was honest, more than her mouth. Just the brief touch had lit little fires inside her, bringing her recalcitrant body to life. For a minute, she rested back against the wall, breathing evenly. When she was pretty certain she had herself under control, she straightened and headed back into the living room. Jenny and her mother were at the window, and she joined them there. Together they watched as Logan slung his leg over the Harley and pulled on his helmet. He gave a brief wave in their direction, the engine rumbled to life, and he vanished off down the road.

They all let out a sigh in unison.

"Well, that was intense," her mum said. "But I like him. He's…different."

"He is indeed."

Jenny turned to her. "Mum, can I have a tattoo?"

She looked at her daughter through narrowed eyes, but knew well enough not to give an outright no. "Maybe when you're older."

"How much older?"

"About sixty-five. Now, why don't you go read for a while? We can talk later."

She watched as Jenny pouted then wandered off to her room. Sinking onto the sofa she exhaled loudly, the tension drained out of her, leaving her weak and wobbly. Her mother gave her one look then disappeared into the kitchen, coming back a minute later with two glasses of wine.

"Here," she said, handing Abby one and sitting down beside her. "You look like you need this." She took a sip and grinned. "So, Logan. He's…stunning."

"I know."

"Well, don't sound so depressed about it."

Abby shrugged. "I'm not looking for a boyfriend. And if I was, he'd be way out of my league."

"Yet you slept with him the other night."

"Mum!"

"That's not a criticism. I've been worried about you. You need more fun in your life."

"Ha. Bad things happen when I have fun."

"Jenny happened."

That stopped Abby in her tracks. She'd always thought of that one-night stand as a disaster that should never have happened. But if she could turn back the clock now, she would do it all over again. Jenny was worth everything that had happened. The only bad thing had been her mother and father splitting up—she'd always hold herself responsible for that. Even losing the chance to study law was a secret blessing. Deep down she'd only done it to please her father, to follow in his footsteps. Really, from an early age all she'd wanted to be was a detective, and she was close to that now. Hah, how would Logan feel about the fact that she'd only joined the force because of him? She must remember to tell him sometime.

"I know, and I wouldn't have things any other way. But getting involved with Logan is not a good idea. I get the impression he's not really into relationships—more a one-night stand sort of guy."

"Or a two-night stand in your case"

"Thanks for reminding me. But my point is, a relationship between us won't last, but hopefully his with Jenny will. If we start something and break up, it will make things awkward. Better if I keep my distance from the start and keep things between us on a sensible footing."

"Good luck with that. But sweetheart, I have to be honest, I don't look at that man and think 'sensible.'"

"No."

"Just ask yourself one thing—do you trust him with your daughter's happiness?"

"I hardly know him."

"You know him well enough. Otherwise he wouldn't be here."

Her mum was right. If she hadn't trusted Logan, she would never have told him. She would have walked away. Her work had given her a good insight into character, though, honing a natural instinct. And strangely, despite his bad-boy appearance, she did trust him. And she was glad he hadn't tried to turn himself into something different to impress them today. She'd probably have been less trusting if he'd turned up in an estate car and wearing a suit. This was Logan; he wasn't going to magically turn into perfect father material overnight. Jenny would have to accept him as he was and that looked as though it was happening.

"Yes, I trust him."

Trouble was, she wasn't so sure she trusted herself.

Chapter Seven

Abby punched her pillow and slammed her head back down. It was after midnight, but she couldn't sleep. Jenny had taken an age to settle. She'd been hyper and hadn't stopped talking about Logan. She'd wanted to know everything about him, asking question after question, which were all a little difficult to answer because Abby knew virtually nothing about him or his family, except he had a brother with a nipple ring and a father who hated the police. She'd have to make him a questionnaire. Maybe she could email it to him so they wouldn't have to meet. She was guessing she wasn't his favorite person right now.

But it wasn't that keeping her awake. It was that damn kiss. Short and not particularly sweet, she couldn't get it out of her head. The feel of his firm lips on hers, which made her think about where else those firm lips had been. The other night he'd tasted her everywhere. No one else but Logan had ever done that for her and it had been…unforgettable. Her insides melted at the memory, a now-familiar little pulse beating between her thighs.

He wasn't even here and he was driving her wild. Her nipples were hard beneath the strappy camisole she wore over her pajama bottoms. She bit down on her lip as she ran her palm over the tight little peaks and felt the touch between her legs. She imagined Logan's mouth there, sucking and pulling, and she wriggled against the mattress.

It was no good. If she didn't do something she would never sleep. Closing her eyes, she stroked her hand from her breasts down over her belly, slipping it under the waistband of her pajamas. Then lower, imagining it was Logan's hand, Logan's fingers sliding between the folds of her sex. God, she was wet. She touched her clit lightly, then harder.

The phone on her bedside table rang and she nearly jumped out of her skin.

Who would phone her at this hour?

She had an inkling, as though she had conjured him up with her fantasies. She pulled her hand free, sticky from her own juices, and picked up the phone with her other hand. "Yes?"

"Abby?" Of course she recognized his voice; it was imprinted on her memory. Right now it sounded low, growly, sexy as hell, and tingles zinged up and down her nerves.

She swallowed. "Yes."

"I want to see you."

She shook her head, trying to clear her mind. "To discuss Jenny? We can talk tomorrow."

"No, not to discuss Jenny. Not to discuss anything. There's only one thing I want your mouth doing right now, and it isn't talking."

"Oh." An image flashed in her mind: her on her knees in front of Logan, his cock, hard and ready and right in front of her face. She licked her lips but couldn't think of anything intelligent to say.

"So?" he said as the silence drew out between them. "Are

you going to let me…see you?"

"When?" What had happened to keeping her distance? She was so weak willed.

"Now would be fucking good."

"Now? It's after midnight and I'm in bed—"

"There'll be time to sleep when you're dead, baby. Get your ass out here."

"Out here? Where are you, Logan?"

The sound of a car horn startled her. For a second she thought it was from the phone, then she realized the noise originated right outside her house. She scrambled out of bed and shuffled across to the window, drawing back the curtain. A black pick-up truck was parked at the curb. The headlights were off, but in the light from the streetlamps she could make out Logan lounging in the driver's seat. He raised a hand in her direction.

Her mouth went dry and her pulse raced. She put the phone back to her ear. "What the hell are you doing here, Logan?"

"I was sitting at home, just me and Grunt, and I started thinking."

"Thinking about what?"

"You and me. And a few of my more persistent fantasies. A minute later I had my hand down my pants and my fist around my cock, and I was imagining your mouth doing all sorts of interesting things. And I thought—fuck this. I want the real thing. So here I am."

Be strong Be strong. "Well, you can go away again. I'll talk to you tomorrow."

"Not going to happen, babe." The horn sounded again, and across the road a light went on.

"Will you stop that? You'll wake the neighbors. And Jenny."

"Come out then, and I'll stop. Come on, Abby, where's

your sense of adventure."

"Bloody hell," she muttered.

Would it be so bad? Just once? After all, hadn't she been doing the same thing, pleasuring herself while imagining Logan doing all sorts of wild and wicked things to her? Now here he was.

"Don't you have a fantasy or two?" he murmured and she gripped the phone tighter. "I can make them come true. Anything you like. You only have to ask."

Oh God, he was like the devil tempting her. She took a deep breath. "I'll be down in five."

She ended the call before he could say anything else. Grabbing a pair of jeans out of the wardrobe, she pulled them on over her pajama bottoms, added a zip up sweatshirt over her camisole, shoved her feet into flip-flops and was ready to go. She ran her hands through her hair but didn't bother with any other preparations.

After closing her bedroom door gently behind her, she tiptoed down the stairs. Everything in the house was silent. She snatched her keys from the sideboard and was about to open the door when a voice spoke from the top of the stairs. "And where are you going at this time of night, Abigail Parker?"

She stopped stock still. Her mother stood at the top of the stairs, wrapped in a dressing gown, hands on her hips.

"I...er... Oh God." She couldn't think of a single thing to say.

Her mum raised an eyebrow. "Well, just practice safe sex...this time." And she was gone.

Abby considered heading back to bed and hiding her heated face under the pillow, but Logan would no doubt beep until the whole neighborhood was awake. She let herself out of the house and headed down the drive and through the gate. The passenger door to the truck was open and without giving herself time to rethink the decision, she hauled herself inside and plonked herself down on the leather seat.

"Nice truck," she muttered, giving Logan a quick sideways peek. He'd changed into faded jeans that clung to his long legs and lean hips and a white T-shirt. He appeared big in the confines of the cab, filling the space. His hair was loose around his shoulders and disheveled as though he'd run his hands through it. Her fingers itched for her to do the same.

"It was my ride before I went inside," he said, switching on the engine. He glanced at her and gave her a quick grin. "More than a few of those fantasies of mine actually took place in this very truck."

"Really?"

"Yeah. So did I wake you up?" he asked pulling out onto the empty road.

"No." She shifted on the seat as she remembered what she'd been doing when he'd called. She cleared her throat. "I couldn't sleep. I was…"

"You were what?" Another quick glance. "Did you know you're blushing?"

"No, I'm not. And where are we going?"

"Somewhere quiet. I didn't think you'd want to make out in front of your house."

"God, no." She could imagine her mum peering out from behind the curtains. And was that what he was here for? To make out? It made them sound like naughty teenagers sneaking off. It also made her hot and wet, everything tingling. She pressed her thighs together to try and alleviate the sensation but it just intensified. "Is that what we're going to do? Make out?"

"Hell, yeah." Logan rested one hand on the leg nearest him, steering with the other. Sliding it up her denim clad thigh, he pressed his fingers into the apex between her legs, pushed upward, and the tingles turned to sparks. How could he do this to her so easily, with just the simplest of touches?

Finally, he turned the truck into an alley off a quiet residential road, pulled up, removed his hand, and switched off the headlights and the engine. He sat back for a moment, staring straight ahead, then twisted in his seat so he was facing her, his expression serious. "So, what were you doing when I called?"

"Nothing…thinking."

"Thinking about me?"

"No."

"Liar."

"Okay maybe a little bit." Like his mouth and hands.

His heated gaze played over her in the dim light, finally returning to her face. "You're blushing again. Tell me what you were really doing."

No way.

"Come on, Abby. I told you. Turnabout's fair." When she still didn't speak, he swiped his tongue over his lower lip. "How about I help you out? Were you touching yourself? Did you get all hot and wet thinking about me?"

She gave a quick nod.

"See that was easy. Was your hand between your legs when I called? Were those naughty fingers of yours in your wet pussy?"

She nodded again.

"Shit, that's fucking hot. Did you get yourself off?"

She shook her head. "You interrupted me."

"Good. When you come, I want to be the one calling the shots." He reached out and trailed his hand down over her cheek. "So you're feeling pretty needy right now?"

She was going to explode with embarrassment. "Can we not talk about this?"

He grinned but nodded. "I guess we have better things to do. So this next fantasy—you're the secretary again—and you've fallen even harder for me, so you help me escape."

"Really? That's impressive."

"Babe, you're one pretty resourceful woman. Anyway, you meet me outside with my truck and…" His gaze focused on her lips, and she remembered what he said about there only being one thing he wanted her to do with her mouth and it wasn't talking. She could make a pretty good guess at what he did want, and her tongue came out to lick her lower lip. A flash of amusement flickered in his eyes. "I think you can guess what happens next."

She glanced down at the soft faded denim hiding the huge bulge in his jeans. He was already hard, that much was clear. She licked her lips again, and he groaned.

Could she do this? Here and now, on the side of the road? Did she *want* to do this? *Oh yes*. She just wasn't sure of the logistics. Should they undress, should she wait for him to make a move? But for once she wanted to instigate things, wanted some level of control.

She peered up at his face. His eyes held a hint of frustrated amusement, but he remained silent as if to let her think things through. She could do this. And she wanted to do this.

Reaching out slowly, she trailed a hand over the bulge of his erection, heard the hiss of indrawn breath. She slipped her fingers under the hem of his T-shirt, pushed it up, and fumbled with his belt buckle, finally managing to tug it open. She hesitated a moment, then flicked open the button at his waist. No going back now. Taking the zipper tab between her finger and thumb she slowly lowered it. He groaned. "Baby, don't you dare stop."

Now what?

She tugged at his jeans, and he lifted up so she could pull them down around his hips. His boxers snagged on his erection, and she took a deep breath and slid her hand inside, wrapped it around the rigid heat of his shaft, pushing his boxers down with her other hand.

She gazed down at him. The other night had been too intense; she hadn't really taken him in. Now she stared. She'd never thought of penises as beautiful before, but Logan's was stunning. Satin skin stretched tight over steel. He was long, reaching up past his navel, and thick, flaring at the head, and her sex clenched up at the sight of all that masculine power at her mercy.

Her mouth watered.

Suddenly his seat fell back, and she realized he'd pulled the lever beside him. Now he half lay beside her. Should she stay in her seat or kneel on the floor? She'd try the seat first— she didn't think she'd fit on the floor.

"You're making me hurt here." His voice was ragged with tension.

"I'm sorry," she muttered. "Was I quicker in your fantasy?"

"Hey, don't make me beg."

She cocked her head on one side and studied him. "Would you?"

"Hell, yeah."

She was so wet from just thinking about this. Lowering her head, she stroked her tongue from the base to the tip, swirling around the head, breathing in the musky scent of him, her senses filling with the clean taste—citrus and soap and hot man. She pulled back and glanced up. "Is there any particular way to do this? You know…to fulfill your fantasy?"

He growled low in his throat. "You're a tease, Sergeant Parker."

Was she? She never had been before, but she was different with Logan. He was so…carnal. She felt liberated when she was with him like this, free to be someone she'd never even thought existed. She'd worry about it later; right now she had more important things to do.

This time, she took the flaring head of his cock fully into her mouth and sucked, loving the way his hips lifted, trying to push deeper into her mouth. She grazed him with her teeth, and he went still. She was in charge here. Slowly, she slid her lips down over the length of him, until he hit the back of her throat and she could take no more. She'd heard about deep throating but suspected she might throw up if she tried, and that might ruin the moment. Wrapping her fist around the base of his cock, she spent minutes gliding up and down the thick shaft, then more, suckling the head, feeling him jerk and pulse inside her mouth. She loved that she could give him pleasure like this. A quick glance showed his eyes were closed, his lips slightly parted, and a ragged pulse beat in his throat.

She kissed the tip and moved lower, using her tongue to caress the taut skin of his balls until they gleamed wetly and she knew he was close. Wrapping her mouth around him again, she concentrated on the head, sucking hard, then soft. His hand slid into her hair, fingers digging into her scalp as he guided her movements. She reached between them, cupped her palm around his balls and squeezed gently, and he came with a final thrust into her mouth, filling her with the hot, salty taste of him. She swallowed convulsively as he pumped into her. She'd never actually swallowed before. Her partners in the past had always pulled out—out of politeness she presumed. She liked this way better.

Finally he collapsed back onto the seat. She pulled away, giving him a last quick kiss, and lay her head on his belly while he stroked her hair from her face.

"Holy shit, that was better than any fantasy."

She smiled against his skin and pushed herself up. His face held a sleepy, sated expression, his eyes half-closed. A weird sensation ran through her, the need to hold him tight, to not let him go, but she shook the feeling away. His T-shirt was pushed up, his jeans pushed down, but he made no move to cover himself. Unable to resist, she reached out and stroked the silky hair that bisected his belly, twirling her fingers in the curls. His stomach was rock hard, the individual muscles clearly visible beneath the olive skin.

"Take your jeans off," he said, the words jolting her from her appreciation of his body. As she considered it, she grew hotter, wetter. She glanced at his cock, still semi-hard, but she doubted he was capable of performing right now.

"Can you…?"

He grinned. "Not yet—you've drained me dry. But I fancy playing a little. Take them off."

She glanced outside but the street was dark and quiet. Nothing moved.

Why not?

She was sure there was a very good reason. And she couldn't quite believe she was considering it—little miss perfect, never put a foot wrong, was going to get next to naked with Logan McCabe in his truck. Before she could change her mind, she undid the snap on her jeans and wriggled out of them, taking her pajama bottoms with them, shoving them onto the floor at her feet.

"And the top."

That would leave her in nothing but the lacy camisole she slept in. She shrugged out of the jacket and dropped it on top of her jeans.

"Christ, that's hot. Come here."

"Come where?"

"You ever made out in a truck before?"

"Never."

"What a surprise. Come over onto my seat, straddle my hips."

She gave him a look of disbelief, but shuffled over. Logan placed his hands on her thighs to help her and soon she was kneeling, one leg on either side of his hips, feeling extremely vulnerable. Logan obviously liked it, his cock twitched and jerked, coming alive once more. His gaze played over her body like a flame.

"Touch yourself," he murmured.

"What?"

"Stroke your pussy. Show me how you were touching yourself when I phoned. Come on, sweetheart. It's hot. Shy? I'll go first." He fisted his hand around his cock, and her mouth went dry.

Slowly her hand shifted to between her legs. The heat pooled in her sex, sliding down her inner thighs, she was so turned on. She caught her lower lip between her teeth as she pushed one finger between the folds, sliding it over her swollen clit. Looking into his face, she found him staring at where her hand was buried between her thighs, while his own hand pumped his cock. Shivers of sensation ran through her, coalescing in her belly, sinking lower…

"Are you wet?" he asked, his voice husky with a need that amped up her own desire.

She withdrew her fingers to show them glistening with moisture. He grasped her hand and brought it to his mouth, his tongue licking at her fingers so she felt the touch between her legs. God, he was sexy.

"More," he urged.

This time she used both hands, one to spread her lips, the other to stroke herself then push inside. The pleasure was building. She couldn't believe she was doing this. He dragged the straps of her camisole down over her shoulders and arms, tugging it down to free her breasts. Her nipples were hard little peaks, and he rolled one between his thumb and fingers, tugging. The sensation was enough to tip her over the edge, and she came apart, pressing the heel of her hand against her sex to prolong the pleasure.

Finally she went still and peeked at him through half-closed lashes. His cheekbones were flushed, his breathing ragged.

"Can you reach into my pocket?"

She fumbled around until she found what she was looking for and pulled the condom from the back pocket of his jeans. Obviously, if nothing else, the last ten years had taught him safe sex. He took it from her, ripped open the packet with his teeth, the rolled the condom over his erection. "Now where were we?"

Placing his hands on her hips, he shifted in the seat until his cock nudged at the entrance to her body. Then he pulled her down, impaling her on the thick, hard length of him, and she closed her eyes and gave herself up to the sensations.

She didn't know what time it was when he finally pulled the truck up in front of her house. They'd made love, and then they'd talked, about Jenny mainly, for hours. He wanted to know everything. Afterward, they'd made love again. Now they were both dressed, but the cab reeked of sex, thick and musky, reminding her of the things they had done. Things she wanted again already.

Would she ever get enough of him?

Whoa! Scary thought.

She was pretty sure that for Logan, she was a novelty: his fantasy girl. But he wasn't the monogamous type, and he'd tire of her soon enough. She would do well to remember that, because it would be so easy to get hooked, and she would be in for a fall if she allowed herself to get addicted to the way he made her feel.

She should step back now before it was too late.

He switched off the engine, jumped out, then came around and opened the door. The small courtesy surprised her, but she clambered down. After what they'd shared, she didn't know what to say, so she decided to say nothing. As she turned to head to the house, he stopped her with a hand on her arm.

In the light from the street lamps, he appeared serious. "We need to talk."

"I know."

"You're not working tomorrow. Meet me for lunch."

It was her day off, but how did he know she wasn't working? Something to find out later, when her brain was functioning better.

She nodded.

"I'll pick you up here at one."

"Okay."

The skin on her back prickled as she walked up the drive, the hairs on the back of her neck rising. She shut the door behind her and peered through the glass, waiting until he got in the cab and drove away.

Her body was replete, sleepy, and she tiptoed back to bed. This time she was asleep as her head touched the pillow.

Chapter Eight

If they were going to talk they had better be somewhere public. It was the only way Logan could guarantee he'd keep his hands off Abby. His fantasy girl was turning out to be addictive. But they needed to sort out how far she was willing to let him into his daughter's life.

The thought pricked at him. He was still pissed off at her for not telling him sooner, although the blow job had gone a long way to earning his forgiveness. Hey, so what—he was shallow. And if the blow job wasn't enough, the sex afterwards had been out of this world. His dick twitched at the memory.

He'd gotten her to touch herself again while he fucked her, and she'd come screaming. He'd had to clamp his hand over her mouth so she didn't wake the neighborhood. He grinned at the memory.

Now, he gave her a sideways glance as they followed the restaurant hostess to their table. It was hard to believe she'd let herself go like that. In fact, looking at her now—it was almost impossible. She was so…perfect. She wore a navy blue skirt suit with a white silk shirt and two inch heels. Her hair was back in that bun thing and he had the urge to reach across and pull it down around her shoulders. Her makeup was minimal, and she wore small pearls in her ears. Her looks screamed "boring."

But she wasn't. Underneath that prim exterior was his wild woman, burning to get out. What had turned her this way? Was it having the baby alone? Or had she been like that before Jenny? He tried to remember back to that one night they'd had together eleven years ago. She'd been everything he ever fantasized about in a girl. Even before prison. Beautiful, full of life and laughter. And she'd wanted him, had melted in his arms.

Never underestimate how much of a turn on it was to be desired. She'd stared at him across the room as though he was the most beautiful thing she had ever seen. He'd been powerless to resist.

"Your table, sir." The hostess held out a chair for Abby, and Logan seated himself opposite—out of reach. No touching until the talking was out of the way.

He ordered a bottle of wine and sat back, fingers tapping on the table as he studied her, trying to work out what made her tick. "Tell me," he said. "That night, eleven years ago. Why did you have sex with me? I'm guessing it wasn't usual behavior for you." Though he was pretty certain she hadn't been a virgin—he'd have noticed. Wouldn't he?

She pursed her lips as if deciding what to say. Not a good sign. "I was drunk. For the first and last time."

What the fuck?

"You're telling me the only reason you had sex with me was because you were drunk." He could hear the outrage in his voice. And he'd been thinking she'd taken one look at him and fallen wildly in love. Yeah, what fucking fairy tale was he living in? But it was clear, from his instinctive reaction, that that's exactly what he'd believed...or hoped.

She nodded solemnly. "Sorry, but it's the truth. It was my eighteenth birthday. My friends organized it. We were supposed to be going out to dinner, or at least that's what my parents thought. It wasn't even my dress—they bought it for me as a birthday present. I would never have gotten something like that on my own."

"I remember," he said. It had been black and sparkly and hardly there, showing off her long slender legs and a vast amount of cleavage.

"You would never have even looked at me if I'd been dressed in my own clothes."

God, even she thought he was shallow. But maybe she was right.

"Anyway. I drank tequila. Lots of it. And then I saw you…"

"Across a crowded dance floor. How romantic."

"Actually you were. You were perfect. My birthday present. All that night I felt like I was someone else, in a bubble that the world couldn't touch." She bit her lower lip as if unsure whether to go on. "You made me feel so good. It was the best night of my life."

Okay, he forgave her for the drunken part. "Mine, too." It was the truth. Maybe for him it was partly because of all the shit that came afterward. That night had been something good to remember.

"And then I woke up on that sofa in your office, and your dad walked in, and my bubble well and truly burst."

He grinned. "I've never seen anyone dress so fast. You were gone before I could even ask your full name, never mind your number."

"There was nothing to stay for. That night was time out. We came from different worlds. I did my best to forget you and get on with my life, until I found I was pregnant and…" She gave a shrug, but he was guessing it hadn't been a good time.

"It's hardly the stigma it used to be."

"You don't know my father."

The waiter came with their wine and poured them both a glass. They studied the menu for a few minutes. "Have you been here before?" she asked. "What's good?"

He decided not to mention that he owned the place—part of his diversifying-out-of-nightclubs plan. "The steak is very good if you like meat—it comes from an estate in Scotland."

"You don't like meat?"

"I'm a vegetarian," he said. "Much to Grunt's disgust— no bones in the house."

He ordered the stuffed peppers while she chose a medium rare steak.

"What's he like," Logan asked. "Your father, I mean? He wasn't there on Sunday."

"He and mum split up ten years ago."

"Not divorced?"

"No."

"Why'd they split?"

"You met my mother. She's lovely but a little ditzy. They were totally unsuited, but she worked so hard trying to fit in with his world. Then…"

"Then?"

"I got pregnant, and he demanded I get an abortion so I could go on with my legal studies. When I refused, he threw me out. Though I'm pretty sure he only did that because he thought it would bring me in line. And for the first time in her life, my mother stood up to him. Told him she was going as well. And here we are."

So that one night with him had effectively cost her a career and her father.

"I'm not sorry," she said, surprising him. "I wouldn't change things even if I could. I love Jenny, and my father was a control freak. Mum's better off without him."

"Does she agree?"

"I don't know. She doesn't talk about him much, but I think she still loves him."

"What about the law thing—is it what you wanted to do?"

She grinned. "No. I was doing it to please my father. He used to talk to me about his cases, and I'd pretend to be interested, but what I really wanted to do was catch the bad guys."

"Shit." That was scary. "And am I a bad guy?"

She cocked her head and studied him. "I thought so once. But we wouldn't be here if I still believed that."

He took a sip of wine. She hadn't touched hers yet. "Have a drink," he said. "I promise not to take advantage of you."

She lifted her glass and glanced around her. "This place is nice. And I bet I could never afford it on a police sergeant's salary. So…how rich are you, Logan?"

He almost choked on his mouthful of wine. Trust her to come right out and ask. Most women would hint around the subject, but not Abby. Why did she want to know? Was his father right, and she was about to ask him for money? Somehow he didn't think so. "Rich enough to pay toward my daughter's upkeep."

Her eyes widened. She hadn't expected that. So obviously she hadn't been about to demand he hand over vast amounts of cash to support them all. He was glad, but she wasn't going to shut him out of their lives by not allowing him to be responsible.

"I don't want your money."

She sounded almost angry, but at that moment the food arrived, and she clamped her lips tight on whatever else she'd been going to say. She took a swig of wine. As the waiter left, she leaned in toward him. "Is that why you think I told you? To get at your money?"

His lips twitched. He liked her angry. "No. Now eat your food."

He thought she was going to argue, but she picked up her knife and fork and started eating. Logan sat back, ignoring his own food, watching her.

"Good?" he asked.

"Oh yes. Sublime."

He couldn't believe he was getting a hard-on watching her eat. Her mouth, the way she flicked out her tongue, the obvious enjoyment. She'd had the same expression last night with his cock between her lips, as though it had been the most delicious thing she had ever tasted. He shifted in the seat. Now was not the right time to think about blow jobs. He started eating.

When her plate was clean, she put down her utensils, sat back, and sighed. "That was wonderful. I don't get to eat out much, so it's a treat."

"No dates?"

She shrugged. "Sometimes. Not for a while. I've been busy. And it's hard when you have to look at men as potential fathers as well as boyfriends."

"Well, that's not an issue now. Jenny has a father."

"Hmm. But we don't want your money."

A part of him liked that—his fantasy girl had never been mercenary. "Hard luck. I'll pay maintenance. It's up to you what you do with it. And she starts secondary school this year. I'll pay school fees."

"She's going to the local school. It's good and it's what she wants."

"Maybe. Or maybe she didn't have any other options. She does now." He sat back took a sip of wine, studied the mutinous tilt of her chin. "You asked how rich I am. I'm very rich. My father signed the nightclub side of the business over to me when I was twenty-two, and I've increased the value twenty-fold in the years since."

Probably more than that. He might not have Declan's business training, but he had a flair for making money, making the right decisions at the right time, and the business had flourished.

"Was that when you came out of prison?"

He nodded. "Yeah. Rory reckoned I needed a challenge, something to keep me busy and on the straight and narrow." He grinned. "He needn't have bothered—I'd already decided I was never going back to prison. But I enjoy it and I'm good at it. So my point is, I have the money, and I want to pay my share. Jenny is my daughter. You might not like that, but you have no choice but to accept it."

For a moment she looked like she was about to argue some more—her eyes stormy, her face tense—then she took a deep breath and her expression smoothed out.

"You call your father Rory? Why's that?"

He shrugged. "Actually, he suggested it. We didn't really know each other until I was ten. I was a little...precocious, and wasn't quite ready to believe he wasn't the monster my mother had made him out to be. Wasn't ready to call him dad."

"But you get on okay."

"Yeah. We clash a lot—we're too much alike—but he's great. I was screwed up when I came to him, but he straightened me out."

"Not very well."

It took him a second to realize she was talking about his spell in prison. He thought about trying to defend himself, to explain to her what had happened. Tell her it wasn't his fault. But he was betting as a police officer, she'd heard that a thousand times and wouldn't be impressed. Besides he wasn't ready to try to justify anything to her. She had to make her own decisions about what sort of man he was.

"That wasn't my father's fault." Time to change the

subject. "So, I'll talk to my lawyer and get the paperwork set up. You talk to Jenny about schools."

"Okay."

That had been too easy. On to the next thing. "I want to see her alone. I want to get to know her."

She nodded. "I think she'd like that."

So far so good. "I want her to stay over. Every other weekend."

Shock flared in her eyes. She hadn't been expecting that. His little sergeant thought he was going to calmly accept the crumbs she let him have. She needed to learn otherwise. And fast. All part of understanding who he was.

"I'm not sure that's a good idea," she said. "Maybe we can talk about it when she's older."

"What? Like twenty? Never going to happen." He ran a hand through his hair wondering how far to push. But they needed to get this settled between them. "I talked to my lawyer. If I take this to court, I will get access. You want us to go down that route?"

"You wouldn't."

He sat back in his chair and eyed her lazily. She was becoming a little unraveled. He liked that. "Try me."

She bit her lip and a jolt of awareness ran through him, settling in his cock. He'd been doing well at keeping his mind off sex. Now his head filled with images of Abby in various fantasies, pressed up against the wall, her legs wrapped around his waist, his dick buried deep inside her.

He shook his head to dispel the vision. Had she bitten her lip on purpose, to distract him? He didn't think so. For such a sensual woman, she seemed sublimely unaware of the effect she had on him. Well, until they were both naked, then she noticed. It was probably just as well she didn't understand exactly how far he would go to get inside her panties again. Not that he was budging on his decisions about Jennifer. But anything else was negotiable.

"Come on, Abby. My house is hardly a den of iniquity." Okay, maybe he could give a little. "You can always come along the first couple of times. Make sure she's okay, that Grunt and I are capable of acting in a civilized manner."

She did that little nibble on her lower lip again, following it with a swipe of her pointed tongue, and he had to bite back a groan. Finally, she took a deep breath and nodded. "That would be good. At least the first time. For me, maybe more than for her."

He liked that she was being honest. "Thank you."

"I'm sorry if I came across as difficult. Of course you'd want her to stay with you. You just surprised me. I guess I never really thought this through."

No, she'd thought he was the sort of man who'd want nothing to do with a ten-year-old daughter. She was starting to learn different. But they'd had enough lessons for today. He'd gotten what he wanted. Well, some of what he wanted. Would she give him the rest?

"You want dessert?" he asked.

She shook her head.

"You want to come back to my place, and we'll fuck each other's brains out?"

He held his breath as he waited for her answer. If she said no…well, he'd have to try and persuade her. But she pushed back her chair and rose to her feet. "Let's go."

Okay, so she was nervous. This was Jenny and Logan's first solo date. He was taking her to her favorite place—London Zoo. All day, Abby's fingers had itched with the need to reach for her cell phone and find out if everything was going well. So far she'd resisted.

She hadn't seen him since the day they'd had lunch together. She'd used the excuse that she was working long shifts, which was true, and she was too tired for anything else. She'd half expected—okay, half hoped—that he would make another nighttime visit, but nothing. He'd obviously accepted her excuses, which went to show she'd been right to think she was nothing more than a novelty.

She hated the little jab of pain that accompanied the thought.

Accept it.

As promised, he'd taken her back to his place and fucked her brains out. She'd never liked the word but it perfectly described what they'd done. There had been nothing soft. It had been hard and brutal, and she had loved every second.

He'd taken her up against the wall in his hallway, as though he couldn't wait any longer, stripping her of her clothes so she was naked while he was still fully dressed, which she'd found incredibly erotic.

An hour and multiple orgasms later, he'd driven her to pick Jenny up from school, come back to the house, and had tea while he chatted to Jenny and discussed what she would like to do at the weekend, finally agreeing on the zoo.

All while she'd sat there remembering the feel of his hands and mouth on her body.

Everything was slipping out of her control. She was glad it was working between them, but now she had to somehow get a grip. Force herself to see Logan as Jenny's father and nothing else. Before that lunch she'd told herself she was going to maintain some distance with him. And all it had taken was one sentence to melt her barriers. Well, one sentence and an hour of sitting across from him trying not to remember what he tasted like, what he felt like deep inside her.

Still, she shouldn't have gone with him. She was a weak-willed nymphomaniac, at least where Logan was concerned.

But all through that lunch, she'd been unable to get naked Logan out of her mind. She was fixated on his penis. But honestly, as penises went, it was just about perfect. Plus he knew exactly what to do with it. When he was inside her, it was as though she were the only thing in his world; he focused solely on her, fiercely possessing her until she could think of nothing else, either.

Ugh!

She had to stop thinking about him like that. Somehow, they had to find a way they could work with each other on a normal basis. For Jenny's benefit.

She couldn't afford to allow him any closer, because then, when they split—as they must, because they were too different—she would be bitter and twisted, and incapable of playing nice. Right now, she could maybe turn her back on this without too much fallout, but the longer it went on, the harder it would be. Because sex with Logan McCabe was addictive.

Already after six days, her body craved his touch.

She got up restlessly and moved to stand at the side of the window, staring out, willing them to appear. On Wednesday, she was going on a date with Jack. Perhaps that would take her mind off things. Jack was a nice man, and even better, she wasn't obsessing about his penis. Actually, she had no interest in seeing his penis. Was that good or bad?

Finally Logan's sleek black sports car turned into the road and pulled up outside the gate. She glanced at her watch. He was spot on the time he'd said they would be back. Jenny bounced out of the car and ran up the drive. Abby headed to the door and opened it just as her daughter reached the house.

"Hi, Mum." Jenny was positively beaming.

Logan was behind her, strolling up the drive. They were both dressed in black jeans and black sweaters. She hadn't been here when Logan had picked Jenny up; she'd still been at work. She suspected Jenny's choice of clothes might have been influenced by her new father. But standing side by side, they looked so similar, it took her breath away.

Jenny turned to Logan, stood on tiptoes and kissed his cheek. "Night, Dad. Thanks. I'm going to my room," she said and disappeared up the stairs. Abby shook her head and turned back to Logan.

"She has so much energy," Logan said. "I'm exhausted."

"She has that effect. But it looks like you both had a good time."

"We did. I said I'd check with you, but if it's all right, I agreed to take her and her friends roller-skating after school on Wednesday. Is that okay?"

"Well, you're brave man, but yes. Go ahead. I'll mention it to their mothers. You know she just wants to show you off to her friends."

"That's okay. How about you? You want to show me off?"

A shudder ran through her. "God, no."

He went still, and she was suddenly aware she had been less than complimentary. But the thought of Logan together with her friends, most of whom were also colleagues on the force, was a scary one. "Most of my friends are police—you hate the police."

"So I do."

They were both silent for a minute. She wished she could take the words back somehow. Be a little more diplomatic. It was too late now. But if Logan really cared what people thought of him, he would make an effort to look a little less… hot? Badass? Mouthwateringly, panty-soaking sexy?

She couldn't believe she'd thought that. She heaved a huge sigh. She was tired that was all; it had been a stressful few weeks.

"My family would like to meet Jennifer."

"They would?"

"Of course they would. Did you think any different? I thought my place next Saturday night. My stepmom is flying in later in the week, and Declan is flying back with Jess, his girlfriend. My sister Tamara already lives in London, so she'll be here as well. And Rory, of course."

"Lovely," she muttered.

He chuckled. "Actually, he told me to tell you that you don't have to stay away from his son after all."

"Ha. It was probably sensible advice."

"Who wants to be sensible?" He leaned in close so his breath feathered against the skin of her neck. "You know, I've missed your tight pussy wrapped around my cock."

Heat flooded her at his words, wetness oozing from her so she had to hold herself still not to give herself away. "I wish you wouldn't talk like that."

"Liar. You like me talking dirty to you. Your eyes go dazed, and you get this little flush across your cheekbones." His gaze dropped and she peeked down. "Your nipples get hard, and I bet under that prim outfit, you're soaking wet for me."

He read her way too well, and she had an idea that if she tried to deny it, he might feel compelled to prove his point. And if he touched her, she'd fall apart. "Maybe, but it doesn't matter. Look, I don't know how to say this, but, well…"

He took a step back. "Oh, I think you're being very clear. I'm in your life because of Jenny, but I'm not good enough for anything else. Maybe a quick screw when no one's looking, but not good enough to mix with your nice fucking friends."

Oh God, she'd hurt his feelings, and she hadn't even suspected he had any. "It's nothing to do with being good enough. Or nice." She took in the tense muscles, the hands fisted at his side. She'd thought he didn't care what people thought about him, but deep down he had a huge chip on his shoulder. His appearance was a way of saying fuck-you to all the people who had looked down on him while he was growing up. Including, by the sound of it, most of the city's police force.

She sighed. Things could never work out between them. He only wanted her because he was working through those fantasies of his. Deprived of any other females, he'd fixated on her. Otherwise he would never have thought twice about their night together. And fantasies, however exciting, were no basis for a relationship. Her mother might say she needed fun, but she had responsibilities—to Jenny, to her job, to Jack if she started going out with him, even to Logan. "We're too different. Look at us"—she waved a hand between them—"under normal circumstances you'd never look twice at me. And you'll get over this fantasy thing and go back to the sort of woman you usually…" She wasn't quite sure how to finish the sentence so she shut up. From Logan's sour expression, he was far from impressed by her speech anyway.

"My usual women? You mean strippers and lap dancers? Yeah. Perhaps you're right. At least they're honest about what they want." He ran a hand through his hair. "And none of them ever made me feel like a second-class citizen. Jesus, I can't believe I let you do this to me. I'm off. Tell Jen I'll pick her up from school on Wednesday, and I'll be in touch about Saturday." And with that he turned and stalked away.

Chapter Nine

Logan paced the hallway, hands in his pocket.

Through the door into the reception area, Rory stood chatting with his wife, Judith, and Logan's half sister, Tamara. Rory caught his gaze, an amused expression in his eyes. Bastard was finding this funny.

Where the hell was she?

After the way they'd parted last time, he wouldn't be surprised if she cancelled, just to pay him back for being a grouchy bastard. But the strength of his reaction had shocked the hell out of him. He'd thought himself impervious to what people thought about him, and she'd brought him face-to-face with how big a delusion that was. He did care. At least about what some people thought. And he was still pissed off that she believed he wasn't good enough to mix with her goddamned copper friends. As if he'd want to anyway.

All the same, he'd dressed with care today, in black pants and a white shirt. His fingernails were clean, and his hair was pulled back into a neat ponytail. He tried to tell himself it was for his daughter, but he was quite aware he wasn't being entirely truthful with himself.

He closed his eyes and saw again Abby's look of abject horror when he'd asked if she wanted to show him off.

The sound of wheels on the gravel outside dragged him from his less than happy thoughts. She was here. He took a deep breath and strolled to the front door. As he opened it, a small red car pulled up between his dad's Ferrari and Tamara's Porsche. He recognized Rachel in the driver's seat and for a second he thought maybe Abby really had backed out—in which case the party would be delayed while he hunted her down and hauled her ass over here. Then she climbed out of the passenger side, and the tension eased from him.

Dressed in a dark blue pantsuit, with a nipped in jacket that emphasized her small waist and the curve of her breasts and hips, she looked as pristine as ever. Her dark hair was loose around her shoulders, and she hooked it behind one ear as she waited for the others to get out. Jenny emerged from the back and Rachel from the front.

There was a commotion behind him, and Grunt pushed past, hurtled down the stone steps, and hurled himself at Abby. She staggered back under the force, then pushed him down and rubbed his huge head. "Hiya, boy," she murmured. "This is Grunt," she said to Jenny and her mum.

Well, at least she was pleased to see his dog.

"Grunt! Come!" Logan called, and the dog slunk away, casting them one last longing look.

He waited at the top of the steps as they followed the dog, coming to a halt in front of him. He ruffled Jenny's hair and gave her a quick hug. She hugged him back—hard—which made him feel a little better. Turning to Rachel, he leaned in and brushed his lips across her cheek. He gave Abby a curt nod. He was probably being childish, but he wasn't quite ready to forgive her yet.

"Come and meet my family," he said. "Everyone's here

except for Declan and Jess. They've just flown in and are on their way from the airport, but they should be here any minute."

"Oh goody," Abby muttered, not quite under her breath, "more McCabe's."

Ignoring the comment, he led them through the hallway and into the main reception room, where Rory stood beside Judith and Tamara.

"That's your grandfather," Logan murmured to Jenny, as he steered her across the room with a hand at her back. Rory was also dressed in dark pants and a white shirt, but with a matching jacket. He didn't look like Logan's idea of a grandfather. Hopefully, Jenny wouldn't be disappointed in her new family—they were hardly conventional.

All three stopped talking and turned to face them as they approached. "This is Jennifer," Logan said, and he could hear the pride in his voice. He turned to Jenny. "Jenny, this is Rory, my father and your grandfather." He bit back a grin as Rory's eyes narrowed at the comment, but he didn't refute it. "This is Judith, my stepmama, and Tamara, my sister."

"We're delighted to meet you," Judith said. She leaned across and kissed Jenny on the cheek, followed by Tamara.

"Hey, I'm an aunt," she said with a grin. "And you look just like me."

Rory reached across and shook Jenny's hand. "Welcome to the family."

"And this is Abby, Jenny's mother, and her mother, Rachel."

Judith and Tamara each gave Rachel a bright smile, and then turned slightly and regarded Abby frostily. From the conversation earlier, he was quite aware they both believed Abby in the wrong to have kept his baby from him for ten long years. He hadn't made much of an effort to defend her, because it was the truth, and while he could understand why she'd done it, he didn't think he would ever truly forgive her.

Her shoulders slumped a little at the less-than-warm reception, and now—when it was too late—he had the urge to stand up for her. Then she straightened and put back her shoulders. She might appear small and defenseless, but he was beginning to realize she had backbone and didn't need—or want—his protection.

Rory kissed Rachel's hand, which made Jenny giggle, and gave Abby a cool nod. "Sergeant Parker."

She gave him a serene smile. "Mr. McCabe."

"Call me Rory."

Her eyes widened as though she found the idea incomprehensible, but she remained silent and gave Rory another serene smile. It looked as though the effort made her jaw ache.

"Let me get you a drink, sergeant," Rory said. He put a hand on her waist and steered her away from the group. For a moment Logan considered rescuing her, but decided she was more than a match for Rory, and maybe it was time his father discovered that for himself.

Abby didn't want to go with Rory McCabe. She also wanted to tell him that if he called her sergeant again she was going to punch him on the nose. And she couldn't understand where the aggression was coming from. But a drink sounded like an excellent idea, so she walked with him across to a bar, where just about every drink she'd ever heard of was set out.

She'd done a little research on Rory McCabe. While the family company was now totally legitimate, with a stellar reputation—thanks to the hard work of Logan's brother, Declan—that hadn't always been the case. But despite the best efforts of the police, Rory McCabe had never done time.

He'd had a frightening reputation, taking over from his father when he was only twenty-one and somehow managing to hold the company together and make it grow. Somewhere along the way, he'd made the decision to go straight and had applied the same level of ruthlessness that he had to everything else. She'd talked to some of the old-timers who had been around in those days; the dislike between Rory and the police went way back and, by the sound of it, had continued even after the company had gone legitimate.

She'd also looked into Logan's case. The police had been called in to stop a fight. One of the officers had taken a punch in the process, and Logan had been arrested. But from what she could see in reading about the case, the charge was excessive, and as a first offense, she wouldn't have expected Logan to do time. But they had pushed for it, claiming undue force. The punch had apparently put the officer in hospital, but all the same it had left a nasty taste in her mouth—she hated injustice of any sort.

"What can I get you?" Rory asked.

"Vodka and tonic."

He poured her a drink that made her glad her mother was driving. Maybe he was trying to loosen her up a little. She was always careful about the amount she drank and hadn't lost control since that night with Logan.

As she took a sip, she glanced back at Jenny to make sure she was okay. She was laughing at something Logan said, and Abby relaxed a little. She'd lost sight of what this was all about. Jenny. And as far as her daughter went, the whole thing had been a resounding success. Logan and Jenny got on well, and there were the beginnings of real affection on both sides.

"She's fine," Rory said. "Loosen the reins a little."

She narrowed her eyes at him. "She's not on a rein."

"No?" His gaze wandered over her and she didn't think he was too impressed with what he saw.

Like I give a shit.

And there it was again. That little burst of aggression she didn't recognize.

"You're so uptight you're going to snap any moment."

She gritted her teeth. "I am not uptight," she ground out. But honestly, wasn't she allowed to be a little bit uptight considering the situation?

She supposed the problem was that she wasn't used to disapproval. All her life she'd done her best to please people—her father, Jenny, her teachers, lately her colleagues at work—done her best to give them what they wanted from her. Now she felt the first twinge of resentment.

"I know what I see," Rory said. "And you could say I have experience with women like you." He looked back at the group, and she had a hunch he might be referring to his wife. She did seem a little uptight, and hardly what she'd expect Rory McCabe's type to be. Abby wasn't like that, though she was aware she might give that impression. She'd grown up always trying to be the perfect daughter and it was hard to shake off childhood programming. But it was none of his business, and she'd always gone out of her way to make sure that Jenny didn't grow up feeling the same.

"You have no idea what sort of woman I am." Time to change the subject because she had a hunch that Rory possessed the ability to rile her up, and she didn't want to be riled. She'd met men like him before; they poked and poked, trying to get a reaction just to see what their opponent was made of. But she wasn't playing.

She took a huge gulp of her drink and glanced up to find Rory watching, amusement clear on his face. She looked away, and her gaze clashed with Logan's. He stood with a hand on Jenny's shoulder, but his attention was on her, and his eyes were hot. She forced her gaze from him and back to Rory.

"I never thought a son of mine would get involved with

a cop."

She took another drink. Already the alcohol was a buzz in her mind. "Hardly involved. I take it you don't care for the police either, Mr. McCabe."

"Call me Rory. And no. You might say I was inconvenienced a few too many times."

"Yet you were never convicted."

"I knew how to avoid it."

"Pity you never taught your son the same thing."

His eyes narrowed, but then he grinned. "At least you're willing to stand up for yourself, and you're not afraid of me."

She rolled her eyes. "Please. What's to be afraid of?" She allowed her gaze to drift from his feet to his face. "I've spent too many Friday nights manning the cells to be intimidated by an ex-petty criminal with an attitude problem."

Had she really said that? Rory was having an extremely bad effect on her personality.

She waited for his comeback, but he surprised her by laughing out loud. "Believe me, I was never petty. And as for teaching Logan, unfortunately he was caught up in the middle of a time of change, when my dealings with you lot were undergoing some significant alterations."

By "you lot" she presumed he meant the police, and that in his earlier days he'd paid the police off to keep himself out of trouble. She wasn't totally shocked or surprised. The force was a cleaner place now, but there had always been officers willing to look the other way in exchange for a supplement to their salary.

At that moment there was a commotion at the front door. Grunt raced past her and hurled himself at the man who'd entered the room. Tall, with short black hair which looked due for a cut, stubble on his cheeks, gray eyes—this must be Declan, Logan's younger brother.

"The McCabe genes must be strong stuff," she murmured.

"Yeah." Rory grinned. "I can't see anything of you in your daughter."

"Thankfully, she has my super-nice personality," she replied, and he laughed again.

A woman entered beside Declan. She was the most beautiful woman Abby had ever seen—tall, slender, with platinum blonde hair pulled back in a ponytail to show a perfect oval face and dark blue eyes. And just like that, Abby felt short and dumpy and plain. The woman's perfection was marred by a scar which ran down from her eye to the corner of her mouth. The scar only emphasized her beauty.

"That's Jess," Rory said. "She was my son Declan's bodyguard, and now she's his other half." Both were dressed casually in well-worn jeans and T-shirts under leather jackets. "They've been traveling, biking across Europe. They flew back from Greece to meet you and Jenny."

"I'm honored," she said.

"I suspect you might get on well with Jess."

"Why's that?"

"She doesn't like me, either. Come on, I'll introduce you."

Rory and Declan hugged, then he leaned down and kissed Jess on the cheek.

"Hey, it's granddad," she said with a grin.

Rory turned to Abby. "Did I also mention she's a total bitch? Jess, Declan, this is Abby."

Declan shook her hand, but she could see that same wary expression in his face as in the other McCabes. "Nice to meet you."

Jess was less reticent; she stepped closer and gave Abby a hug. "Welcome to the family." She glanced across to the group. "They take a little—okay, a lot—of getting used to, but there are compensations." She glanced sideways at Declan as she spoke and licked her lips suggestively. "Is that your daughter? Wow, she looks like Declan. And Logan of course."

Five minutes later, Abby stood to the side and watched the group interact. Jenny stood surrounded by McCabe men—Logan, Declan and Rory. She might well have been intimidated, but they had obviously welcomed her with open arms, and she looked relaxed and at ease chatting with them. Her mum was talking with Judith and Tamara.

"Rory's an asshole, but you have to stand up to him." Jess had come up beside her, a beer in her hand.

"He told me you don't like him."

"Can't stand him. He once tried to pay me to stop seeing Declan."

"Really?"

"It was a long time ago, but I'm not quite ready to forgive him yet." She studied Abby for a minute. "So, I get the feeling there's a little tension here. Jenny has obviously been welcomed into the fold, but with you I sense a little bit of the cold shoulder."

"I don't think they've forgiven me for not telling them sooner."

"No, I can see that might be a bit of a problem. So why didn't you?"

Jess was certainly blunt and to the point, but Abby preferred that to circling around the subject. "I tried, but he was in prison at the time, so I went away again."

"Oh God, of course, that would have been when he was locked up. A sore point, and not only for Logan."

"Why?"

She shrugged. "Well, both Declan and Rory blamed themselves. Rory because, with his background, the cops were always looking for anything on the family, and Declan because Logan got into the fight to protect his little brother."

"Oh."

"They'll get over it."

"I doubt it." She sounded morose. It was becoming clear

that they really didn't like the police, and maybe they had their reasons. But it was who she was, and she wasn't going to change that, didn't want to change it. A detective was all she had ever wanted to be.

"Why's that?" Jess asked.

"I'm a sergeant in the metropolitan police."

Jess's lips twitched, and she burst into laughter. "Fucking brilliant."

"I'm glad you think so. Rory and Logan were less than impressed. Rory almost accused me of some convoluted plot to set Logan up. I mean, yeah, I got pregnant at eighteen with the sole purpose of waiting eleven years and then weaseling my way into Logan's life, discovering what nefarious practices he's up to, and locking him away—for good this time."

Jess laughed again. Declan and Logan stood across the room and they turned at the sound. Logan murmured something to his brother, and they both strolled over.

Seeing them together made her sigh out loud.

"They're the stuff of fantasies aren't they?" Jess murmured. "X-rated fantasies."

They were so similar, with the same height and coloring, though Logan looked edgier, with a hint of danger. If Declan was a sleek, well-fed leopard, Logan was a panther, lean and mean and hungry.

She might say she wanted nothing to do with him, apart from what was absolutely necessary for Jenny's sake, but that didn't stop her eating him up with her eyes. He added a small swagger to his walk and fixed his gaze on her lips.

Jess was the more beautiful—he'd never met a woman to match her—but his gaze was drawn back to Abby. She had shadows under her eyes. Maybe, like him, she wasn't sleeping. He'd been trying to keep his distance, but he wanted desperately to see her alone. Somehow he had to persuade her it was in her best interests to let him into her pants again.

"What are you two up to?" Declan asked as they came up beside the two women. Declan moved in closer, wrapping his arm around Jess's shoulders and pulling her close. Logan wished he had the right to do the same with Abby, to touch her, hold her, as though she was his. The thought surprised him. He'd never been the possessive type.

"Discussing X-rated fantasies," Jess said.

Logan's gaze sharpened on Abby. "Have you been telling tales, sergeant?"

"No," she snapped.

"Tales?" Jess asked. "What sort of tales."

Abby was glaring daggers at him, so he continued, just to wind her up. If ever there was a woman in need of being wound up, it was his sergeant. He nodded in her direction. "The sarge here didn't tell you she's my fantasy girl?"

"Your what?" Declan asked.

"And what sort of fantasies?" Jess added.

"Definitely X-rated. I met Abby just before I was put inside. You could say she was the inspiration for my nightly entertainment." He gave an exaggerated sigh. "Every night, I'd lie in my bunk and I—"

"Ugh. Stop right there," Jess said putting her hands over her ears. "I don't want to hear any more." She cast a look back and forth between Logan and Abby and smiled. "It's been a pleasure to meet you, Abby. I think you'll be a fascinating addition to the McCabe family. Now, I'm going to go introduce myself to your daughter. I'm an honorary aunt after all. Maybe I could teach her to shoot, or…whatever. Now you two play nice." She dragged Declan away, leaving him alone with Abby.

Turning to face him, she stabbed a finger in his chest. "Did you have to tell them that?"

"Ashamed of me?"

"No, I'm not goddamned ashamed of you. Just because I don't want the whole world to know that you spent your year in prison jacking off to some perverted image of me does not mean I'm ashamed."

"Hey, hardly perverted." He shrugged. "Okay, a few might get a little risqué but I'll work up to them slowly."

"Shut. Up."

"Temper, temper."

She gritted her teeth. "You're just so…aggravating."

"I know. Let's go get you another drink." He waved toward her empty glass. "I think it's actually loosening you up a little."

Her jaw clenched tighter. She was in a temper. He liked it. "I do not need loosening up."

"Have another drink anyway, sergeant." He led her across the room, took her glass from her limp fingers and sniffed it, then mixed her a vodka tonic, added ice and lemon, and gave it back to her.

"And will you drop the sergeant crap," she said, taking a huge gulp. "I love what I do, and I'm not ashamed of it. And I'm not going to try to justify it to you lot just because your dad used to be a totally dodgy bastard."

His lips twitched. "Okay."

"Okay?"

He shrugged. The fact was he used it to remind himself of what she was, so he wouldn't get too caught up in the whole fantasy thing and get carried away. She was a copper with a perfection complex. He was an ex-con who liked things messy. There could never be anything between them except a brief sexual fling. Having said that, he wasn't ready to let go yet. The last few days had made that abundantly clear. He was back to jacking off to fantasies of her, and yeah, maybe they were getting a little perverted. Last night's had involved handcuffs. And it was weird, because if he'd ever considered the whole bondage thing, then it would have been him doing the tying up. But there he'd been, handcuffed to the bed, with Sergeant Abby Parker, naked except for her police hat, riding him hard. He had a twinge and shifted.

"What are you thinking?" she asked, her eyes narrowed.

Jesus, he was a mess. In some ways it would be easier if he could just go and slake his bothersome urges with a more convenient, less complicated woman…or two…and relegate Abby to the role of mother-of-his-daughter. But no one else interested him. Only her.

"Well?" she prompted.

"You really don't want to know."

"I wouldn't have asked if I didn't want to know."

He leaned in close. "Well…I was imagining you had me handcuffed to my bed and your tight little pussy was wrapped around my cock. I was at your mercy…and I was fucking loving it."

Her eyes widened, darkening, and she swallowed then glanced around. "Shut up," she muttered.

He followed her gaze and realized they were the center of attention. "Why," he said. "Do you like the idea?" But she was probably right. This was not the time or the place. And he needed to resist the urge to wind her up when Jenny was around. He didn't want their daughter to pick up on any conflict between him and Abby.

She smoothed her hands down the sides of her pants. "I want this to work with Jenny," she said. "She's already fond of you, and there's no going back. So somehow we need to find a way to make it work between us two as well."

She was voicing his own thoughts, so he'd back off at this point. But the truth was, he wasn't ready to let go of his fantasies yet. He'd have to find a way to get her alone, though he suspected she'd be on her guard now. "I know," he said. "And we will. Let's go see how she's doing. I'd rather not leave her alone with Jess too long."

"Why?"

"She's a bad influence."

Chapter Ten

The party had left Abby down and depressed, and by Wednesday she still hadn't managed to shake the effects. She wasn't sure why and was a little scared to investigate her feelings too deeply.

She suspected that she might be a teensy bit jealous of her own daughter. Logan's family had all been so welcoming. And she was happy about that, really she was. If anything happened to her, the weight of looking after Jenny wouldn't all fall on her mum. Jenny had another family now, who'd made it more than clear that they were delighted to have her in the fold. Judith had even asked Jenny over to New York in the summer, which had pissed Abby off, as she should have checked with her first before issuing the invitation.

Jess and Declan had already flown back to Greece, but Jess had promised to get in touch when they finally returned to the UK. She said they needed to show a united front against the McCabe men. It was nice to think she had an ally of sorts. Tamara, she guessed, was waiting to make judgment.

She'd heard nothing from Logan since Saturday, though

she had been busy working long night shifts. This was the last. After tonight she had a couple of days off, and she needed them. She wasn't sleeping well. Her nights were filled with dreams of Logan, which left her restless and on edge. After his comments at the party, she'd expected him to contact her, to try to persuade her into a few more of those fantasies. She was ashamed to admit it, but she had a real curiosity about those kinkier ones he'd mentioned, and she hadn't been able to look at her handcuffs without a vivid image of Logan flashing in her mind. Very inconvenient.

Now, after four days and nothing from him, she suspected that part of her problem was disappointment and frustration.

She was one sad specimen.

She'd also been avoiding Jack. They'd had a good date last week, and he'd made it clear he would like to repeat the event. But she'd been putting him off. It didn't seem right, dating one man while lusting after another.

Logan had taken Jenny and her friends out after school again today. She'd phoned home and learned everyone had gotten back safely and found Jenny already in bed. Probably exhausted from all the excitement. Had Logan been disappointed she wasn't there?

Probably not. He'd obviously lost interest.

She exhaled loudly. It had been a quiet night. She'd caught up on paperwork and worked on the schedules for next week. After a week doing desk work, she was back on the emergency call team and out patrolling the streets starting Saturday. It was her favorite job and would no doubt take her mind off things.

Half an hour to go. Glancing up from the desk, she felt her breath catch in her throat, her heart stuttering as Logan came through the door. She glanced around to see if anyone else was watching, but they had the reception area to themselves. He'd gone into all out seduction mode. Black leather pants molded his long legs and hips. A black leather jacket gave him an air of menace.

"How long until you finish?" he asked.

"Half an hour." As the words came out, it occurred to her that she should have maybe put him off, asked him what he was doing here, rather than obediently answering him. But he'd taken her by surprise, and her mind had turned to mush.

"I'll be back."

And then he was gone, and she was left staring at the door.

The last half hour of her shift dragged. Finally she handed the desk over to her replacement and headed to the locker room. She showered quickly and dressed in navy trousers, a blue sweater, and boots. She didn't want Logan coming inside again. She wasn't ashamed of him, but she didn't see the point of a long, convoluted explanation as to who he was and how he fit in to her life. This might be a police station, but it was no different than any other workplace when it came to gossip. But Logan was nowhere in sight when she came into the reception area. Her chest tightened. Maybe he'd changed his mind. She waved at her replacement duty sergeant and headed out the door. Outside, Logan leaned against the wall, a lazy smile on his face, and the tightness melted inside her.

"Come on," he said, and she followed him around to the parking area at the side of the building. Dawn was close, though the sky was still dark.

"Oh no," she muttered as he approached the gleaming black Harley. No way was she going on that thing.

He turned to her with a grin. "Where's your sense of adventure?"

She held back.

"Actually," he said, "Jenny asked for a ride. I told her I had to clear it with you first. So I'm here to show you how safe I can be."

No way was Jenny going on that monster. But butterflies were fluttering in her belly, little tingles of excitement zipping up and down her nerves. How long was it since she did something wild? No, best not to go there. It all led back to Logan.

He held out a helmet to her. "Come on, sarge, you know you want to."

Tentatively, she inched a step closer, reached out, and took the helmet from him. Before she could change her mind and tell herself that this was a really bad idea, she pulled it over her head. He considered her for a moment then slipped out of the leather jacket and handed it to her. "It can get cold."

"What about you?"

"Oh, I'll be warm enough."

She pulled on the jacket, still heated from his body, and hugged it close, breathing in the scent of leather and spice and warm man.

"Good girl," he said, pulling on his own helmet. "Just sit behind me and hold on tight."

He swung his leg over the bike and patted the seat behind him. She took a deep breath and edged closer. The seat wasn't high, and she managed to get her leg across. Tentatively she slid forward so she was pressed up against him, the *V* of her thighs tight to his ass, and heat washed through her. He turned to the side, no doubt so she could hear him through the helmet. "Try to relax and go with the movement of the bike." As he switched on the engine, vibrations shuddered through her core. Her arms wrapped around his waist so the whole front of her body was pressed up against his back. Her breasts swelled; her sex flooded. He revved the engine and she pressed even closer. Then they were off.

At first she held herself tense, her hands gripping his hard abs through the material of his shirt. But his driving was smooth and assured. They were deep in the city, and though there was little traffic at this time of day, the speed limits were low. Finally she relaxed enough to appreciate how close they were. She loosened the grip of her fingers and splayed them across his belly, feeling the rock hard stomach beneath her palm. She couldn't resist, and one hand slid lower to push under his shirt and onto the hot satin skin beneath. He tensed a little and then relaxed. She dipped into his navel then into the silky line of hair that ran down lower.

He released one hand from the handlebars and placed it on top of hers, pushing it downward over the leather to rest on the bulge at his groin. It pulsed beneath her palm. Oh God, he had a hard-on. Was that dangerous? But she couldn't prevent her fingers from tracing the shape of him. Then he pushed her hand back up, and at the same time they accelerated. She peered around; they were out of the city now and on a wide open road. Logan picked up speed and they were flying. Resting her head against his back, she gave in to the fabulous sensation of riding through the dawn on a Harley, wrapped around a stunning bad boy. She threw back her head and laughed.

He slowed and peeled off the road onto a smaller side street, finally pulling up around the back of a huge warehouse. The place appeared deserted. As he switched off the engine, her heart started up a slow steady thud. She suspected she was about to discover another of those fantasies.

Was it possible to make love on a motorcycle? She still had her hands wrapped around him, under his shirt, palms flat against his stomach. She didn't want to let him go, but she also wanted a kiss—*craved* a kiss. Reluctantly, she slid her hands from him, reached up, and tugged off the helmet. Logan did the same and swung his leg over and stood up. Taking the helmet from her, he placed both of them on the ground next to the bike, then he climbed back on, facing her this time. His hand slid under her hair at the back of her neck, tipping her face up to his. He was so beautiful he made her heart ache. She held herself very still, and time seemed to slow. His lips touched hers, gentle at first, then firmer, his hands tightening in her hair, his tongue pushing inside her mouth, and she lost herself in the taste and feel of him. She hardly noticed as he slid the jacket from her shoulders. He cupped her breasts, his thumbs rubbing over her nipples, his mouth still on hers. Sensation shot from her breasts down her belly to settle at her core. His hands slid down to her thighs, and he lifted her legs, wrapping them around his waist. For a moment she wobbled and her hands gripped his shoulders. He raised his head.

"Okay?"

She nodded. "Is this one of your fantasies?"

"Not yet. This is just a little foreplay." His hands moved to her ass, fingers digging into her buttocks, and dragged her snug up against the huge bulge in his jeans. She tightened her legs around him, rubbing herself against his truly impressive erection as she melted on the inside. With a groan, he kissed her again, molding their bodies close together so her breasts pressed against his chest.

Finally, they ran out of oxygen, and he raised his head. A dull flush darkened his cheekbones, and his hair hung loose around his face—she must have pulled it free at some point—and his eyes glowed almost silver.

"Let's move." He pulled away from her, stood, then picked her up and carried her across the space to the warehouse, putting her down in the shadows of a deep doorway.

"This seems an odd place for a fantasy. Are you going to tell me the details?"

He waved a hand around the area. "This was the closest I could get. So the fantasy is…I'm in the exercise yard at the prison and there's this gang of bad guys who are about to have their evil way with you."

"What am I doing in the exercise yard?"

A look of mock irritation flashed across his face. "Maybe they smuggled you in. Or you got lost and wandered in."

"Over the ten-foot-high wall topped with razor wire?"

"Hey, you're here, accept it. And you're naked. Totally fucking naked. So the clothes have to go." He tugged her sweater over her head, pressing a hard kiss to the skin above her bra.

"You know this is a little far-fetched right?"

"Maybe." But he didn't sound too put out by her skepticism. He reached behind her, flicked open the catch on her bra and peeled the cups from her breasts. Stepping back, his gaze roamed over her, hot and dark. "Boots," he said.

She glanced down and kicked off her boots. He opened the fastener of her pants, slowly lowered the zipper, and pushed them down over her hips and thighs. She shuffled out of them, leaving herself naked while Logan was still fully dressed. The sky was lightening around them, daylight close, and she was naked.

"What next?" she asked.

He studied her, head cocked to one side, lips curved in a slight smile. "Well, you're tied up, your hands above your head."

"Never going to happen."

"I somehow thought you might say that. But we'll work with what we've got." He took a step closer, his fingertips trailing lightly down her arms, sending tingles zinging along her nerves, before catching her around the wrists.

For a second it occurred to her that she was in a deserted place with a man she knew very little about except that he was fixated on her sexually and fantasized about her being tied up and at his mercy. But only for a second. She trusted Logan. God knew why, but she felt safe with him. Well, maybe safe wasn't the right word. Her body thrummed with anticipation, her breasts ached, and a pulse throbbed between her thighs. She knew she was soaking wet and she didn't protest when he pulled her arms up and clamped them together in one of his.

"Shit, that is fucking hot. Your breasts are fucking amazing like this." He wrapped her fingers around something metal. She peered up; a thick metal hook was embedded in the wall above her head. "Can you hold them there?"

She nodded…swallowed…licked her lips. "What happens next?"

"I go to untie you, and you tell me to wait. You're so turned on by me saving you that you can't wait and you beg me to fuck your brains out. Right here and now."

"I bet I don't say that. Even in a fantasy."

He leaned in a little, stroked a finger over her breasts, rolling one nipple between his finger and thumb, tugging it as he watched her face. The action resonated between her thighs, hot and liquid. "Don't you want me to fuck your brains out, sergeant?" he murmured in her ear, his warm breath feathering her skin. "Fuck you hard and fast up against the wall until you come screaming."

Her traitorous sex clenched up tight at his words, and her mouth went dry. His hand shifted to his belt, and he slowly unbuckled it, opened the button on his pants, and lowered the zipper, letting out a groan of relief. His shaft sprang free, rock hard and vertical. She couldn't drag her gaze away as he fisted his erection. "You want this? All of it, deep inside you?"

She closed her eyes for a second. When she opened them, he was focused on her face, his hand still around his cock. As she watched, he squeezed hard, a shudder running through him. Oh Lord, but she wanted him inside her, like she'd never wanted anything before. And all she had to do was beg. She could do this.

"Please, Logan…"

"Go on."

She bit her lip. "Please will you fuck my brains out?"

"Good girl." He grinned. "And because you asked so nicely…"

He pulled a packet from his back pocket, tore it open with his teeth, and rolled the condom down over his erection. Stepping closer, he thrust one leather clad thigh between hers, pushing her legs apart. His big hand cupped her sex, one finger sliding between the folds. "Christ, you're always so wet." His hands shifted to her hips, gripped her hard, lifting her slightly so she grabbed his shoulders for balance.

"Hey, put those hands back. You're supposed to be tied up," he growled. "Trust me, I've got you." She grasped the metal loop again as he shoved inside her with one hard flex of his hips. Her legs wrapped round his hips as he shifted her higher, pushing her back against the smooth metal of the door. He withdrew and she moaned at the exquisite drag of his flesh against hers, then moaned again as he pushed back inside. "So tight and hot and wet for me. All for me." He pressed his face into the curve of her neck. "Ready?"

For what?

But she gave a quick nod, which he must have felt. "Good."

He drew back and slammed into her hard, filling her, stretching her. She had no time to analyze the sensation because he was moving fast. Eyes closed, she clung to the metal above her head as he pumped into her, each fierce stroke driving her higher, pressing against her clit, pushing her beyond the limits of a pleasure that bordered on pain, until she was aware of nothing but the thrust of his hard cock. Inside her everything was building, tightening, growing almost unbearable in its intensity, until at last she burst into a thousand pieces, multicolored lights flashing behind her closed lids. As the pleasure waned, he rotated his hips, grinding against her clit, and she came again.

As she screamed his name, Logan released the last of his control. His head went back as his orgasm engulfed him, flooding his system. Each time the pleasure subsided, she'd twitch her hips, and it would start all over again, until his legs were trembling and sweat beaded his skin.

Grabbing her hips, he held her still. "Christ, no more."

He rested his forehead against hers, and they stayed like that for what seemed like an age. Never in his life had he felt like this. All mixed up, and choked up, and not wanting to let her go. Sex had always been just that—a necessary release of tension. This was way more, and the thought scared him. He'd never wanted more, wasn't even sure what "more" entailed.

She shifted, and he sighed against her skin and raised his head. Her eyes blinked up at him, dazed and sleepy. He wasn't the only one affected by their encounter.

"Thank you," he said.

She opened her mouth, then thought better and closed it again. He'd made her speechless and he liked that. Her hands still gripped the hook above her head as if she couldn't let go, and he reached up, uncurling her fingers from the metal. "You can let go now, sweetheart."

She dropped her hands to his shoulder as her legs gave way, and he wrapped his arms around her. Holding her against his chest, he backed up and slid down the wall behind him so he was seated on the ground with her, soft and clinging in his arms. He'd never liked clingy women, but Abby was different. He closed his eyes and breathed in the scent of flowers drifting up from her hair as he stroked lazy circles on her skin.

After a few minutes, she raised her head, and he found himself staring into fathomless blue eyes. They were filled with an expression he couldn't quite define, but which set off alarm bells somewhere deep inside. Alarm bells he ignored. Right now he felt too mellow. "You okay?" he asked.

"Yes. At least I think so. That was…"

"Intense?"

She gave a wry smile. "That's one word to describe it."

How about mind-blowing? But maybe it hadn't felt the same for her. A car drove past on the road beyond the warehouse, and she shifted in his arms. "You can let me go now," she said.

Time to move and get back to real life.

He sighed. He liked it right here. Real life had a way of tarnishing things. But he uncurled his arms from around her.

Totally naked, she scrambled to her feet and stood. He couldn't take his eyes from the smooth curves of her body. Perfection. She cast him a quick peek as if realizing he was watching, then looked purposefully away. Her clothes were scattered on the ground, and she quickly grabbed them up and pulled them on, only looking back at Logan when she was fully dressed. He was still seated on the ground, back against the wall, legs stretched out. Now he pushed himself to his feet, fastened his pants, and was ready to go.

"I'll take you home."

"What is this place?" she asked as they headed back to the bike.

"A work in progress. I bought the site to open a new club."

He took the drive back a little slower. The roads were still quiet this early, but he felt no urge to rush. He liked the way she held him loosely, but with her breasts pressed against his back.

At that moment, he became aware of a sound. A police siren. He looked in the mirror and swore under his breath. He so didn't need this right now. But sure enough, there was a patrol car coming up behind them, flashing its lights for them to pull over. They were the only thing on the road, so it must mean them, though he hadn't been speeding.

He glanced back over his shoulder, just to check, and then slowed the bike and steered to the side of the road, where he pulled over and switched off the engine. The police car drew up behind. Through the mirror, he watched the officer climb out and approach them.

He turned to the side so Abby could hear him. "Stay here," he said. "I'll deal with this." She did as she was told, not even removing her helmet, and he was guessing she wasn't too keen on being recognized. She probably knew most of the police in this area.

Logan took a deep, calming breath and pulled off his helmet as he swung from the bike to stand facing the officer. The man was young; they were usually the worst, out to prove something. Logan kept his face expressionless.

"Nice bike," the officer said. "Is it yours?"

Like he was going to say no. "Yes."

"You can prove that?"

Logan made a snorting sound, but he turned to Abby who was still wearing his jacket. "My wallet is in the inside pocket."

She reached inside, pulled out the wallet, and handed it to him. He took out the paper and passed it to the officer. Everything was in order. The guy could be as difficult as he liked, but there was nothing he could get Logan on. He just had to wait it out. It wasn't as though he wasn't used to this.

Beside him, Abby's fingers were tapping against the leather of the seat as the officer took an age to look at the papers. Then he glanced across at Logan. "I'm going to call this in."

Logan gritted his teeth but managed a casual shrug. "Go ahead."

"No, wait," Abby snapped, irritation clear in her voice. She pulled off the helmet, and her hair fell loose around her shoulders. "Is there a problem, Officer West?"

So she did recognize him. Logan didn't know whether to laugh or warn her off. From the expression on her face, he probably wouldn't succeed in the latter. She looked pissed.

The man turned to her, a frown drawing his brows together at the interruption. Then he actually looked at her and went very still, his eyes widening, like a rabbit caught in the headlights.

This time Logan couldn't quite stifle his snort of amusement.

Officer West swallowed. "Sergeant Parker?"

"Obviously. You were going to phone something in. What exactly?"

"Um. Er…"

She raised a brow.

"There have been a number of bike thefts recently. We've been told to keep an eye out."

"Fair enough. I take it there's a problem with Mr. McCabe's paperwork?"

He swallowed again, glanced down at the paper in his hand, then back at Logan. "No problem." He handed it to Logan and cleared his throat. "Drive safely." Then he walked back to his patrol car, got in, and drove off.

"Asshole," she muttered.

Logan chuckled. "You're fierce when you're pissed off, Sergeant Parker."

She turned from glaring after the police car to study him. "And aren't you? Pissed off, I mean. There was no reason to pull you over and no call to make a big deal out of it once he'd seen the paperwork."

"No point in being pissed off." He grinned. "I'm not saying you're all assholes, but there are enough. If prison taught me one thing it was to stay cool. I swore ten years ago when I got out, that I was never going back. So I smile and I nod and I make sure my paperwork is in order."

She shook her head. "I'm impressed."

"Good, I'm impressive. Now, let's get you home. You must be exhausted."

Chapter Eleven

"Are you going to tell me why I'm hearing a whole lot of rumors about you?"

She glanced up from her desk and considered ignoring Jack's question and finishing up her application form instead. A vacancy had come up in the detective bureau, and she was going for it. This was all she'd wanted since she'd joined the force, and finally it was within her grasp. She'd passed the exams a year ago and had been waiting for a suitable opening.

But she supposed Jack had a right to ask. They hadn't repeated the date yet, and to be honest, while she was sleeping with Logan—or if not sleeping, then fulfilling his sexual fantasies—she didn't feel she could date anyone else. But Jack was a friend, maybe more, and she owed him honesty at least.

Except she didn't want to talk about Logan.

He was nobody's business but hers.

"I have no idea." She should have known that prick West wouldn't keep his mouth shut. She'd been getting strange looks since she'd come on duty last night, but only Jack was brave enough to ask her outright.

He perched on the edge of the desk. "Rumors involving you, a Harley, and Logan McCabe in the early hours of yesterday morning. I might have discounted them, except I know for a fact that you know McCabe. What's going on?"

"It's nothing to do with work."

"So what is it to do with?"

She pursed her lips while she decided what to say. Logan was in their lives now, and she was convinced he was here to stay. He'd made it very clear he planned to be a big part of Jennifer's life. That wasn't something she could, or even wanted to, keep a secret long-term.

"Logan is Jenny's father."

He rose to his feet and stood staring down at her. "What?"

"Logan McCabe is Jennifer's father." She pressed a finger to her forehead wishing the conversation was over. Or better yet, that it had never started. "He didn't know until recently, and I'd really rather you kept it to yourself for now."

"So how did he find out?"

"I told him of course."

"Why? Why now?"

She drummed her fingers on her desk as she considered her answer, finally deciding on the truth. "Lately Jenny has been asking a lot of questions. And I always felt bad about not telling him. And I sort of expected that he wouldn't want anything to do with us."

"I take it that's not the case?"

"No. He wants to be part of her life. They've met and they get on incredibly well. She's also met his family."

"Rory McCabe?"

"And Declan, and Logan's sister and stepmother."

"Jesus." He ran a hand through his hair. "I can't believe this. Do you really want a man like that in Jenny's life?"

Gritting her teeth, she dredged up Logan's advice. Stay cool and smile. She forced her lips into a semblance of a smile, though couldn't quite make it reach her eyes. "I checked before I went to see him. He's not been in any trouble since that first time. Otherwise I would never have told him. Everyone makes mistakes."

"He's an ex-con. People like that never change."

She picked up a pencil and tapped it on the desk as she tried to control her anger. The pencil snapped. Crap. She didn't recognize herself these days. She never got angry, things never fazed her, yet she was ready to stab Jack with her broken pencil.

"You know absolutely nothing about him. And he's Jennifer's father, so I'd be pleased if you didn't say anything like that in my presence again. Logan paid for whatever crime he committed."

She really hoped that would finish the conversation, but he stayed where he was, looking down at her. "I thought we had a chance together. That there was something between us."

And now she felt guilty. *Great.* "I thought so, too. I'm sorry, Jack. I'm just at a strange place in my life right now. Jenny needs me and…"

"And you're seeing Logan McCabe."

"I am not *seeing* him. Well, not like that." *And it's none of your goddamn business anyway.* But she kept the words to herself.

"So what were you doing in the early hours of the morning with him?"

Breathe slowly and think nice thoughts. Christ, if Logan could do it, so could she. "He was giving me a lift home after my shift finished. Though that's really none of your business."

He shook his head. Again. "You're making a mistake getting involved with McCabe." He waved a hand to the computer screen. "And it won't do your chances of getting into the bureau any good."

"Why the hell should it have anything to do with the

goddamn bureau? My private life is exactly that—private."

"Don't be naive, Abby. It's who you know that matters. It always has been, and I'm telling you—Logan McCabe will drag you down." Then he turned and walked away.

She watched his retreating back as she mulled over his words. Could Logan really hurt her chances of becoming a detective? Part of her wanted to deny that it could have any effect, but as Jack had pointed out, she was being naive.

Sometimes she hated the way things were.

She was good at her job, and she'd make a great detective, and that should be all that mattered. Putting Jack from her mind, she finished the application form, took a deep breath, and hit send.

When she got home an hour later, Jenny had just left for school. Her mother was drinking coffee at the kitchen table and glanced up with a smile. "You look tired."

"I am. I'm going to go to bed."

"Could we talk for a few minutes first? There's something I need to tell you."

Abby sank down into the chair, searching her mother's face. As far as she was aware, her mum wasn't due any check-ups for another two months, and she'd seemed so cheerful lately. "There's nothing wrong is there?"

"No, nothing like that. I'm fine. Sorry, I didn't mean to worry you. This is something else. Nothing bad, I just…"

She got up, poured Abby a coffee, and slid it across the table to her. Abby cupped the mug in her hands and waited. Whatever she'd said, there was something wrong—her mum was pacing the room. "Sit down and tell me."

She sat opposite, pursed her lips, twiddled a finger in her hair, and said, "I'm going back to your father."

"What?" Whatever she'd expected, it hadn't been that. Abby hadn't had direct contact with her father in years, and she knew deep down that she was still bitter about him and his ultimatum. She wasn't sure she would ever forgive him. No way would she ever have considered an abortion, but if her mum hadn't sided with her things would have been very difficult. "I didn't even know you were seeing him." Her mother had kept very quiet about that.

"I went to see him after I got the all clear from the cancer. It was weird, but I really wanted to see him before that, and I'd been thinking about it for a while, but I couldn't do it while I was ill. Afterward…well, I thought, why not? Life's too short to hold grudges, and I loved him. Still love him. What he did was wrong, but he thought he was doing the best thing for you."

"And he's asked you to go back to him?"

"He asked me straight away. I couldn't leave you and Jenny then, but things are different now."

"How are they different?"

"Well, you have Logan."

"I do not *have* Logan." Her head was pounding. She pulled out the pins that held her hair in place and ran her hands through it, pressing her scalp. "Jenny has Logan."

"But he's going to be there for you. You won't have to shoulder everything alone. And he told me his lawyer is drawing up a maintenance agreement, so money will be easier."

Something occurred to her. "Have you been wanting to go back to him all this time but stayed away because of me?"

"Honestly, I never thought about it. It wasn't an option, and I was very angry with him for a long time." She was silent for a minute, but Abby was aware there was more to come. "He wants to see you and Jenny."

"Does he?"

"He knows he made a mistake, a huge mistake, but he's sorry."

"Really?"

"Don't be cruel. He's paid for that mistake. I won't ask you to see him, but I would like you to. I'd like us to be a family again."

Abby sipped her coffee and traced a pattern on the table with her fingertip. "This is such a surprise," she said finally. "I knew nothing about it. Why didn't you tell me?"

Her mum shrugged. "You had a lot going on, and I knew you'd…disapprove. You see everything in black and white, and you can be very unforgiving."

That made her sound truly horrible. She didn't want to be like that. "I'll see him, and I'll take Jenny."

"You needn't worry. I'll still be around when you need me to look after Jenn. She can sleep over at the house when you're working nights and she's not at Logan's. Or…"

"Or?" Abby prompted.

"Or you could move back with me. Both of you."

She thought about it…for all of two seconds. While she was ready to let her father into their lives, no way was she going to live with him again. Just the thought of Jenny having to experience the stifling atmosphere she had grown up in made her shudder. "I don't think that would work."

Her mother smiled. "Maybe not."

"You'll be okay? You won't let him bully you?"

"I'll be fine. He's changed. He missed us all."

Could people change? Her mind flew back to Logan. The thing was, she didn't want him to change. She liked him just the way he was. Liked him too much. That wasn't the problem. No, the problem was that he would never fit into her life, and he would probably never want to. He wasn't the settling down type, he was the lets-have-some-fun-and-say-good-bye type, and with Jenny in the picture that wasn't an option.

So it was up to her to be the sensible one.

And she was so fed up with that.

It was his daughter's first sleepover. Jenny had been so excited about her new bedroom. Logan had told her she could decorate it any way she liked and she'd been talking non-stop through dinner about her plans. Now she was tucked up in that bedroom, falling asleep as soon as her head hit the pillow.

As they closed the door behind her, he turned to Abby. She was staying over as well, and he'd had hopes that she wouldn't be using the spare room he'd set up for her. He knew they needed to be discreet around Jennifer—no screaming— but he could manage to be discreet with the proper incentive.

What he didn't think he could manage was another night without her. It was becoming increasingly obvious that he was addicted to his fantasies and his fantasy girl.

He slipped an arm around her waist, but she shrugged it off and walked down the hall, leaving him standing there, watching her go. A frown tugged his brows together.

He'd been distracted by Jenny's excitement, but now that he thought about it, Abby had been distant all evening. She'd hardly spoken a word directly to him. His frown deepened and he rubbed a finger down his chin. He didn't think he would ever understand what was going on inside her head. Maybe that was part of the attraction. Though he did wish he could get a glimpse of her thoughts right now.

He'd believed they'd come to some unspoken agreement that morning at the warehouse. He wanted her. She wanted him. They were fucking fantastic together. His dick gave a little twitch of agreement. Now, she was obviously having second thoughts, or third, or…whatever. He was beginning to doubt he'd be acting out any fantasies tonight, unless it was on his own. He groaned. He couldn't believe how much he wanted her. Needed her even. When had that happened?

He followed her slowly down the stairs. She headed back

to the kitchen and started to clear up, and he leaned against the door watching her for a minute. He liked seeing her in his house. but he wanted her attention right now. They obviously needed to talk, if that was the only way to find out what was on her mind.

"Leave that," he said. "My housekeeper will do it in the morning."

She turned, a small frown on her face. "You have a housekeeper?"

"Yeah. She looks after the place and walks Grunt."

"Of course she does." She dried her hands and turned to him. "I might go to bed then."

He'd shown her to the spare room when she'd arrived. But he was damned if he was going to let her disappear there now. "It's only nine o'clock."

"I'm tired."

"Well, a glass of wine will help you sleep." He crossed the room and grabbed a bottle of red from the rack. When he turned, she looked on the point of bolting. "We need to talk."

Her brows drew together. "We do?"

He got the corkscrew from the drawer and opened the bottle. "You obviously have something on your mind."

"I have?"

He lifted up the bottle. "Come and talk to me. Like normal people. You can tell me what's bothering you, and I'll give you my expert advice. And afterwards…"

"Afterwards?"

"We can talk some more. Unless you'd like to do something else."

For a moment he thought she would say no, but she gave a quick nod. "Okay. There is something I want to say."

That didn't sound good, but at least she wasn't going to bed and leaving him alone. He led the way into the lounge and saw her glance briefly at the chair where he'd fucked her that first time, before she sat herself primly on the edge of the sofa, knees together. She was in navy slacks and a white shirt tonight. One day, when she loosened up with him a little more, he was going to take her shopping. Get his wild girl back.

He poured two glasses of wine, handed her one, and sat down beside her, keeping a little space between them. Not because he wanted to, but he sensed she might walk out if he crowded her. They were quiet as she sipped her wine. When the first glass was gone, he leaned across and poured her another. He hadn't taken a drink of his own yet. Finally, she relaxed back and heaved a huge sigh.

"What's the matter?" he asked.

"Nothing really."

"Come on. Spill it, Abby."

"I spent the whole of last night's shift pretending I didn't notice everybody whispering about me. And I didn't manage to sleep today. I'm just tired."

"Why were they whispering?" Though he had a pretty good idea.

"You know why. That prick West told everyone about seeing you and me."

"Ignore them."

She turned to face him, head tilted as she studied him for a moment, clearly not particularly liking what she saw. Then she drank some more wine before speaking. "I know you don't care what people think about you, but I've worked hard to get where I am. I've earned their respect."

And being seen with him would hardly enhance that. And he wasn't naive enough to think it didn't matter. It could make her life difficult, and that pissed him off. He had an urge to go punch them all in the heads, but that would hardly help anyone. "They'll soon forget, or find someone else to talk about."

"Maybe." She tugged on a loose strand of hair. "I'm

applying for a place in the detective bureau, and someone suggested that my relationship with you might hinder my chances."

"And what did you say?"

"That we didn't have a relationship. That you were Jenny's father and that was it."

His eyes narrowed on her. "So fucking up against a wall in the early hours of the morning doesn't constitute a relationship."

She bit her lip. "I've upset you again, and I really didn't mean to do that."

"No, it just seems to happen all on its own."

"This isn't about you, it's about me. You're...so comfortable with what you are and I've always struggled to fit in. But I'd succeeded, finally, and now..."

"And now screwing around with me is making you look bad. You know, image isn't everything."

"I do know. It's just I've wanted this for so long. Anyway, it's not your problem, and I'll work it out."

She didn't seem convinced, was still worrying away at her lower lip with sharp white teeth, and he wanted to lean over and soothe her with strokes of his tongue, kiss her until she forgot about all those assholes she worked with. Until she forgot everything but him. He dragged his thoughts away from that road, not wanting to frighten her off. At least now she was talking to him, even if he didn't particularly like what she had to say. And he was guessing there was more. That small frown still marred her forehead.

"Something else gone wrong?" he asked when she remained quiet.

She flashed him a glance. "Not wrong exactly." She took another sip of wine and another deep breath.

"Come on, sergeant. You know the old saying—a problem shared is a problem halved."

Her lips almost curled into a smile at that. "It's not a problem. It might actually be a good thing. I just haven't wrapped my head around it yet."

"Around what?"

"My mother and father are getting back together. She's moving in with him."

"What about you?"

She quirked a brow. "What about me?"

"Are you and Jenny going with her?" He didn't want her to. It was none of his business, but he didn't want anyone else looking after them but him.

"No. We'll stay in the old house. Mum has said she'll babysit whenever I need her. We'll be good."

He didn't think, just opened his mouth and words came out. "Perhaps you and Jenny should move in here." For a few seconds he was shocked into silence by his own speech. He'd never invited anyone to move in with him before. Never even come close to wanting to. But when he thought about the idea, he liked it. It felt right.

That way, even if the physical relationship with Abby petered out—and he couldn't imagine that right now—then he would still have her close. They could be friends. He'd never had a woman friend before; he wasn't a particularly friendly guy, but he could make it work. He'd make the effort for Abby and Jenny. They might not be a real family, but they would be together and that was important. He'd spent his first ten years hardly knowing his father. He understood the importance of family.

"Are you out of your mind?"

Her words dragged him out of his rose-colored vision of the three of them playing happy families. He watched her warily as she slowly placed her glass on the table in front of her. She clearly wasn't enamored of his offer, definitely wasn't jumping up and down and squealing with joy at the idea of sharing a house with him.

"It's a big house, so why not? You could have your own room," he offered. He'd actually envisioned her sharing with him, at least at first, but that might be a little optimistic. Best not to crowd her. On the other hand, he wanted her with him. "Or we could share, at least until one of us wants some space."

She stared at him, brows drawn together as though she were translating his words from some weird foreign language but they made no sense at all. "*Completely* out of your mind?"

He ignored the warning signs and kept right on going. Excitement was shooting through him. Something told him this was the way forward, an opportunity he shouldn't throw away. "We'd get to spend time together, and I'd get to spend more time with Jenny without taking her away from you. Come on, Abby, think about it…it makes sense."

She shook her head slowly. It was dawning on him that she wasn't experiencing the same sense of anticipation he was. From the tension radiating from her small body, she wasn't feeling anything good at all. "It makes absolutely no sense at all. You're crazy if you think I'd move in here with Jenny. I told you seeing you could seriously damage my career, and what do you do—ask me to move in with you. Yes, of course it makes sense—if you're a complete moron."

He opened his mouth to say something—what, he wasn't sure—but she beat him to it. "Jenny needs a stable environment, not to live with some adrenaline junky who happens to have a—very probably short-lived—sexual fixation on her mother."

"You want something permanent?"

She gritted her teeth. "Of course I don't want anything permanent."

"Or is it that you just don't want anything permanent with me?"

She glared at him. "You know what? Maybe you're right.

Maybe it is just you." She sighed and ran a hand through her hair. "Sorry, that was uncalled for, but you bring out the worst in me. Come on, Logan. We've only really known each other a few weeks, but you do not come across as the sort of guy looking for commitment. Yes, it might be fun for a while. You'd get to play out your fantasies, and I'd have the best sex ever. But what happens when the fantasies run out, or you start fantasizing about another woman. What if you want to bring her home?"

"I wouldn't do—"

"Wouldn't you? How long do your relationships usually last? A month? Three months? Are you saying I'm different? You want to marry me, Logan? Give Jenny a real family?"

He had no clue what to say to that. Not that he seriously believed she wanted to marry him. She was simply making a point. And making it very well.

He'd *never* thought in terms of marriage. The word sent ripples of fear down his spine. Now he tried to get his head around the alien idea. Obviously he took too long, because she stood up.

"I thought not," she said. "I'm going to bed."

This time he made no move to stop her.

Had he really asked her to move in?

And had she really asked Logan to marry her?

God, she'd seen real fear in his eyes.

She shoved her head under the pillow and hoped the world would disappear. It didn't. Light filtered in through the curtains, but everything was still quiet in the house.

Last night she'd thought he might come after her, attempt to continue the conversation, and she'd lain awake for a long time. Finally the slam of his bedroom door along the hallway hinted that he wasn't coming. That should have settled her, but she'd tossed and turned. When she finally fell asleep, it was only to land in the middle of a nightmare—Logan making out with the stripper she'd seen him with that time at the club, all fake red hair and huge fake breasts. Abby had tried to run away, but somehow she was handcuffed to the bed. "You wanted to marry me," Logan had sneered in her dream. "Do you really think a man like me will be satisfied with someone like you?"

She punched the pillow. God, she was screwed up and a total goddamn cliché. And now she felt tired and cranky and she had to go to work. Jenny was spending the day with Logan, and no doubt they would have a fabulous time together without her, because she was a miserable, boring bitch.

Anyway, it was Logan's fault. How could he have asked her to move in, especially after what she'd just told him? She was quite aware that, once again, she had totally overreacted. But then, Logan had that effect on her, made her behave in ways she had never thought she would, like some sort of bad-tempered, uncontrollable harpy.

Who'd asked him to marry her.

She didn't even want to marry him. He was totally unsuitable husband material. He'd never fit in with her lifestyle or her friends.

Except he was doing a pretty good job of being a father to Jenny.

And she'd hurt him. She hadn't thought she had that power. But her reaction to his proposition had come as a shock to him. Maybe he was used to women who would jump at the chance. And if she was honest, if it wasn't for Jenny, perhaps *she* would have jumped, taken what she could get of him, for as long as she could, and dealt with her broken heart at the end of it. But Jenny was there, and Abby knew now that if she allowed herself to get in any deeper, the inevitable breakup would be that much harder, and she needed to be able act as though it didn't matter—for Jenny's sake. Which meant living with him was not an option.

In fact, from now on, she was maintaining a distance. She'd let this go way too far.

The sound of a door banging told her that someone was up. Time to go out and face the day. She struggled out of bed and into the shower. The water revived her a little, though not enough. She tugged on clean clothes, but she couldn't be bothered with makeup or doing anything fancy with her hair so just pulled it up into a ponytail.

Voices drifted out from the kitchen as she came downstairs. She hesitated, took a deep breath, and pushed open the door. The voices stopped as she entered. Jenny was at the table still in her pajamas. Logan stood at the stove with his back to her, dressed in faded jeans and a gray T-shirt. His feet were bare. In her black pantsuit, she felt the odd one out. So what was new?

"Dad's making bacon and eggs," Jenny said.

She nodded, sinking down opposite her. What she really needed was coffee, lots and lots of really strong coffee. She could smell it somewhere, and she glanced around, her gaze finally settling on the coffee pot across the room. She was pushing herself up as Logan turned. He brought a plate of food and placed it in front of Jenny. It looked perfectly cooked—she was impressed.

"You can cook?" she said.

He gave her a cool look that told her he hadn't forgiven her for last night. "What? You think a man like me wouldn't be able to cook?"

She flashed him a warning look—she didn't want Jenny picking up any of their bad vibes—but Jenny giggled. "Mum can't cook anything but toast, and she usually burns that."

Logan grinned. "Really. Little Miss Perfect can't cook?"

Jenny giggled again, while Abby gritted her teeth and forced a smile.

"You want some?" Logan asked.

Her stomach churned at the thought. "Just coffee, please."

He crossed the room, poured her a mug, and placed it in front of her. She hung her head over it and breathed in the fumes.

Last night, she'd avoided speaking to him over the dinner table while Jenny acted as a buffer between them. This morning they didn't need a buffer. He was pretty much ignoring her, and after ten minutes, she could sense Jenny's puzzled glances between the two of them. This was what she'd worried about: that any altercations between her and Logan would spill over on Jenny. Their daughter wasn't stupid.

But this morning she didn't have the strength to fight it or make it better. She gulped down the coffee, burning her mouth in the process, and stood up. "I need to go to work." She crossed to Jenny and dropped a quick kiss on her head. "You have a good day, and I'll see you tonight."

"Okay, Mum."

Logan followed her out into the hallway, and her heart sank. She didn't need this right now. Grabbing her bag, she made for the door. He halted her with a hand on her arm, and a shiver ran through her. A simple touch and her body came alive. She stopped and turned slowly.

His expression was cool. "I just want to say you can relax. I'll back off. You've made it clear you want nothing to do with me. We'll need to pretend to be friends for Jenny's sake, but I won't push you for anything else."

She bit her lip. She should be happy, but heat was rolling through her, and her eyes pricked. She had to get out of there before she made a total fool of herself. This was what she wanted. Accept it and get out.

"Thanks," she muttered.

For a second, she thought he might say something else, but he nodded and turned away. Abby let herself out of the house, blinking away the tears.

She never cried.

It was messy and uncontrolled and just not her. But she drove the car out of the drive, around a corner, and pulled up on the edge of the road.

And bawled her eyes out.

After five minutes, she sniffed and pulled the tatters of herself together. She had her mum, Jenny, a great career, and maybe a new job to look forward to. There was no reason to feel like everything was over.

Chapter Twelve

Logan pulled up in front of the house and sat for a minute, fingers drumming on the steering wheel. He hadn't seen Abby for a week. Not since the disastrous night he'd asked her to move in with him.

He missed her.

And it wasn't only the sex, though God, he missed that. He missed her company. He liked her, and he'd spent an inordinate number of hours trying to work out why. What was there to like? She was uptight, screwed up, and thought he wasn't good enough.

Maybe he *wasn't* good enough.

Not for her and her impossibly high standards, anyway. And he never would be. So there was no point in trying. He'd save himself a whole load of pain if he accepted that now. Because if he got in any deeper with her, and she turned her back on him…

The muscles in his gut tightened. Christ, it wasn't as though he had a good track record; his own mother had dumped him in exchange for a paycheck. However crappy a mother she had been, he'd loved her, and he never wanted to go through that again. There was probably something about him... Shit, he was getting maudlin.

The one thing he could do was offer his daughter unconditional love. She would never feel the way he had.

He hadn't seen Jenny since the sleepover, either. Today they were going out for lunch, but he was hoping he would get a few minutes with Abby first. Not that he had any clue what he was going to say to her. He just wanted to see her, hear her voice.

Was he losing it?

Probably.

He got out of the car and headed up the drive, but when the door opened, Rachel stood there, and his heart sank.

"Hi, Logan, you want to come in? Jenny is getting her things."

He followed her into the lounge and stood shifting from foot to foot, feeling like a teenager in front of his girlfriend's mother. Except Abby wasn't his girlfriend. Finally he could hold back the question no longer. "Is Abby around?"

Was that pity flashing across her face? Was he so fucking obvious?

"I'm afraid she had to go in to work early." She smiled brightly. "So how are you and Jenny getting along?"

"Good," he said, but was saved from any more polite conversation by Jenny appearing at the door.

He couldn't believe the extent of his disappointment. He'd done such a great job of not seeking her out this week, and he'd looked on today as his reward for good behavior. But it wasn't Jenny's fault, and he forced a smile. "What would you like to eat?"

"Pizza."

"Pizza it is."

"Dad?" she asked as they drove through the city.

He cast her a quick sideways glance. He recognized the tone now—she was about to ask him something and wasn't sure what sort of answer she would get. "Yeah, sweetheart?"

"Before we go to lunch, can I see where you work?"

He hesitated. What was the right answer? While he was proud of what he'd achieved with the clubs, he didn't think they were a suitable place for a ten-year-old. On the other hand, he didn't want her to think something bad went on there, or that he was hiding something.

Christ, it was difficult knowing what was right. Maybe it was all about finding a balance. He took a deep breath. "It's not a place for children, but how about we park the car there and you can take a look from the outside."

"Okay."

He blew out a breath. Not so bad. "So have you decided about school next year?"

"I think I'm going to stick with the local one."

"Is that because all your friends will be going there?"

She thought for a moment. "Partly. Me and Mum spent some time looking at different places. We even looked at boarding schools—there's one where you can take your own pony."

"You don't have a pony."

"I know. It's tragic."

He chuckled.

"But mum's on her own now," Jenny continued. "So I can't leave her. And the day schools I could go to in London don't seem any better than the local."

"No ponies?"

She wrinkled her nose. "None. And the local school has a really good reputation, just as good as the ones you have to pay for, so I don't see the point."

God, she was bright. Had he been that sensible at ten? Somehow he doubted it. "How about riding lessons for your birthday?"

"Really? Can I?"

"Only if your mother agrees." Was he going to get in trouble for this? Maybe he should have checked with Abby first. But at least now he'd have a legitimate excuse to seek her out.

Half an hour later, he drove the car down into the underground parking below the club and switched off the engine. "Come on, let's go find that pizza."

They took the stairs up to street level and out into the alley that ran along the side of the club. It took up the width of one block.

"This is my club," he said, waving a hand at the building. "At least, this is one of them. The first one my dad opened, years ago."

"It's huge." Jenny peered into one of the windows. "I can't see anything. The glass is all dark."

"There's not much to see. Just a big room where people dance."

As they came out onto the main street, where the club's entrance was situated, the big black double doors opened, and Carly—the dancer they had taken on the day Abby had first come here—stepped out. She was dressed in sweats and a tank top, her bright red hair pulled into a ponytail. When she saw Logan, she stopped and gave a huge grin. She closed the space between them, leaned over, and kissed him on the cheek. "Just wanted to say thank you—Jerry took me on permanently last night."

"You deserve it."

"Well, thanks anyway for giving me a chance." She cast Jenny a curious glance.

"This is my daughter," Logan said. "Jenny, this is Carly. She works as a dancer at the club."

Jenny was eying the rose tattoo on Carly's shoulder.

"Hello."

"Nice to meet you, Jenny."

"She's really pretty," Jenny said as Carly disappeared down the street. "Can I be a dancer when I grow up?"

Crap.

What the hell was the right answer to that? Not that he had anything against dancing as a career, but he wasn't so sure Abby would agree. "Perhaps, but it's *really* hard work," was all he could come manage.

She stared after Carly almost wistfully. "Dad?"

There was that tone again. A tic started up in his cheek. "Hmm?"

"Can I have a tattoo?"

Again—what the hell was he supposed to say? "How about we talk about it when you're older."

"How much older?"

What was reasonable? Why hadn't he discussed this stuff with Abby? Probably because they were too busy working through his fantasies to get down to serious topics. That needed to change, because this parenting thing was a minefield. Maybe there were books he could read or classes he could take.

"Eighteen?" He sounded tentative, but he had no clue what the right answer was.

"Brilliant." Jenny grinned, and he breathed out in relief. "Mum said sixty-five."

Crap.

Time to change the subject. "You know, I met your mum right here, in that club."

"You did?"

He nodded. "It was her eighteenth birthday."

"Was she your girlfriend? Is that how you had me?"

It occurred to him—as he wiped the sweat from his forehead—that he'd been getting off easy up to now. His daughter had obviously been saving up the difficult stuff. Explaining what a one-night stand was and how he'd had one with her mother was not an option. "Are you hungry?" he asked. "I'm starving. Should we go get that pizza?"

She gave him a look that made it clear she saw straight through his diversionary tactics, and he scrubbed a hand over his chin. "She wasn't my girlfriend *exactly*, but we did like each other, and I'm sure we would have been if…" Christ, how much to tell her? What did she already know?

"It's okay," she said. "I know you couldn't be with us because they locked you up. Mum told me"

She had? What else had she said?

"And that it wasn't your fault," Jenny continued, as if hearing his unspoken question. "You were just looking after your brother."

Something warm twisted inside him. Abby might not want him in their lives, but she was doing her best to ensure it worked. He made a mental note to say thank you. Another excuse to go see her. God, he was pathetic. "Yeah, that's what happened."

Jenny cocked her head. "I wouldn't mind a brother. Then I'd have someone to look after me. Or someone for me to look after. That would be nice."

He bit back a smile. "You've got your mum and me to look after you. Come here." As he held out his arms, she stepped in close. He hugged her tight for a moment and then kissed the top of her head. "Let's go get some lunch."

A little while later they were seated in his favorite pizza place. They gave their order and he sat back. He'd resisted asking on the way here, but now he couldn't refrain from just one question. "How's your mother?"

Jenny took a sip of Coke then stared him in the eyes. "I think she's avoiding you."

It occurred to him that maybe he should find a safe way

out of this conversation that he shouldn't have started in the first place, but somehow the words just popped out. "She is? Why do you think that?"

"Well, she was supposed to be looking after me today, but she phoned Gran and asked her to come around. She told Gran that work had called and she had to go in, but they hadn't. She could have waited until you'd picked me up."

He had no idea what to say to that, but he didn't have to worry, Jenny was on a roll. "Maybe it's because she's got a new boyfriend."

He looked up, but her expression was guileless. "She has? That's nice," he said, lying through his teeth. A new boyfriend? Christ, she was a quick worker. Unless she was already seeing this new guy while she was screwing him. No doubt he was someone suitable, someone responsible, not a tattooed ex-con with commitment issues.

There. He'd admitted it to himself. He had issues. She was right to stay away from him. And he wasn't going to rise to Jenny's bait. He really wasn't. He was quite aware that Jenny was indulging in a few daydreams of a happy ever after between him and Abby, and while he didn't want to burst her bubble—and he didn't want to think too hard why that was— he didn't want to encourage her either.

Jenny didn't need any encouragement. "His name's Jack and he's a detective. She works with him."

A fucking detective. That was rubbing it in.

"He's nice." Jenny added when he didn't say anything.

"She brought him home?" She'd better not be sleeping with this guy.

"I've met him before—they've been friends forever. But this was different. They went out for dinner, like a proper date."

Ha. So much for not going on dates. What else had she lied about?

The food came and they were silent while the waiter placed their pizzas in front of them. Jenny's was vegetarian as well. Was she trying to impress him? He wasn't hungry, and he was fighting an almost irresistible urge to grill his own daughter for details of her mother's love life. He was a goddamned mess.

"He's not as nice as you though," Jenny said eventually. Perhaps she realized she was being less than diplomatic. "And he doesn't have a motorcycle or a dog." She took another mouthful. "Or any tattoos."

At least his daughter liked him. Or she liked his bike and his dog and his tattoos.

After lunch he dropped Jenny off at the house Rachel was now sharing with Abby's father. It was in Chelsea—a much more affluent part of town than the one Abby lived in—a townhouse, four stories high, and probably worth millions. She'd said her father was a lawyer; he obviously came from money.

"Do you want to come in and meet my grandfather?" Jenny asked as he walked her to the front door.

"Another time," he said, and she leaned up on tiptoes and kissed him on the cheek.

"I think Mum likes you better than Jack," she said as the door opened and Rachel appeared.

Driving away, he tried to shift his black mood. He should be happy for Abby. Hell, his coming into her life probably gave her more time to see other men. She'd said it had been hard juggling her daughter and her career. Well, whoop-de-fucking-doo. She could go fuck some other man while he was babysitting their daughter. Good to know he had some uses even if he wasn't good enough to be her boyfriend.

Was that what she was doing now? Something dark built up inside him at the thought, and his hands tightened on the steering wheel.

Okay. Take a step back.

He was losing it. Again. Since when had he wanted to be anyone's boyfriend? It was entirely up to her who she fucked. Besides, she was at work right now so she couldn't be out with this new guy. Except they worked together. So who knew what they got up to when no one was looking. On fucking taxpayers' time. Hardly ethical. Maybe he should report them to someone.

With that thought, he pulled over to the side of the road and switched off the engine. Running a hand through his hair, he came to the conclusion that he wasn't, in fact, losing it. He had lost it, totally and completely. She was driving him insane. Miss Prim and Proper had him tied up in knots.

He cast his mind back to that night in the lifeboat, when he'd made that vow to go find his fantasy girl. What had he expected? Probably that he'd see her and she'd be nothing like the girl he'd dreamed about, and he could put her behind him…and do what? Go on with his life. Find someone he wanted for more than a few weeks. Because he was quite aware that he'd used his fantasy girl as an excuse to never get close to the real women he dated. They would never measure up to the girl of his dreams.

Everything inside him tensed up at the idea. Abby was right—he didn't want anything permanent; the idea terrified him. But it didn't matter anyway—things hadn't worked out like that. Abby was nothing like the girl he remembered, the girl he'd dreamed about. She was something different, the last type he would expect to go for, yet he couldn't stop thinking about her.

The truth was, they'd both grown up; his fantasy girl had become his fantasy woman, and he didn't want to let her go. But at the same time, he couldn't make himself make that commitment. Not that it mattered because she didn't want him in her life anyway. Not any more than was necessary under the circumstances. He wasn't good enough.

Shit. He couldn't believe that was getting to him. He was rich and successful. He knew a whole load of women who would jump at the chance of sleeping with him. Why did he want the one he couldn't have? Or was it as simple as that? He was going all Neanderthal; he was in this for the chase, and if he did catch her, then what?

She was the mother of his daughter, that was all. There was an unbreakable bond between them. They needed to find a way to coexist.

He'd stayed away from her as he'd promised. But maybe he should go see her, congratulate her on her new relationship, show he had no hard feelings. He gritted his teeth. Just a fucking hard dick.

He could tell her he hoped this new, suitable relationship helped with her career.

Him, bitter and fucking twisted?

Hell, yeah.

As she came out of the door, Abby stopped short. Logan was leaning against the wall outside, arms folded across his chest. He was dressed quite conservatively in black pants and a black shirt, the sleeves rolled up, probably for his lunch with Jenny. But his hair was loose around his shoulders, giving him an uncivilized appearance, further enhanced by the cold, hard expression on his face.

She so didn't need this right now. She'd had a long week, and she wanted to go home and lie in a hot, bubbly bath then go to bed.

Who was she kidding?

She wanted to make love with Logan with a desperation that made it clear she was doing the right thing in keeping her distance. Being apart from him hurt. Seeing him now and not being able to touch him was a physical pain.

Should she ignore him? Walk the other way? But there was a dangerous glint in his eye that warned her not to push him.

What was his problem?

She forced herself to walk toward him, coming to a halt a foot away. "Hello."

She waited for him to reply, but he just watched her silently, his gaze wandering over her, giving nothing away. She shifted from foot to foot then heaved a huge sigh. "What do you want, Logan? Is it something to do with Jenny?"

"Jenny is fine."

When he offered no more, she gritted her teeth and made an effort to relax. *Keep cool and smile.* "What then?"

"Actually, we had a very interesting conversation over lunch."

"You did?"

"We did."

Christ, he was irritating. What the hell could Jenny have said? She searched her mind but came up blank. "And…?"

He pushed himself up from the wall, shoved his hands in his pockets, and she had to fight the urge to take a step back. "She told me you were seeing someone."

A frown pulled her brows together. "She did?"

"Jack."

"Oh." Why the hell would Jenny tell him that? She'd only had the one date with Jack, and that had been two weeks ago. And exactly how much had her daughter told him.

"I take it he's *suitable*?"

He almost sneered the word. She'd really gotten to him, and she was sorry about that, but she never would have dreamed he was the sensitive type. She tried to come up with something diplomatic to say. They were drawing attention, and she wanted him gone. It was the shift change, and a lot of her colleagues were coming and going, casting her glances as they went, making her squirm. She wished she had a little of Logan's imperviousness. He appeared oblivious to the curious stares. But then, he didn't give a toss what anyone thought—apart from her. Oh no, *she* wasn't allowed to think bad things about him. Just everyone else.

She tapped her fingers against the side of her bag as she tried to come up with a plan to get rid of him. What the hell did he want anyway? An introduction? Maybe as Jenny's father he thought he had the right to vet her men friends.

Somehow she didn't think that was his reason. He was being territorial, which, after the way they had left things a week ago, was pretty weird.

They'd been standing without saying anything for over a minute. She opened her mouth, then clamped it closed again as Jack came through the doorway. Great timing. He caught sight of her immediately—or maybe someone had told him she was out here consorting with an undesirable type, and he was rushing to the rescue.

Her head hurt.

She saw the moment Logan noticed Jack coming toward them. His shoulders tensed; his eyes narrowed. He looked from her to Jack, and his jaw clenched. Jeez, he was uptight. She reached out and rested her hand on his arm. "You okay?"

He glanced down at her hand and shook his head, the tension easing from him. He gave a short laugh. "No. I'm a fucking moron."

She didn't have time to answer as Jack came up beside her. "Everything okay, Abby?"

"Why the hell shouldn't she be okay, *Jack*?"

So he knew who Jack was, or he'd guessed. *Great, just great.*

Jack shrugged, but she could tell he was uncomfortable.

She had an urge to sit down, cover her head with her hands, and wait until it all went away. She was getting fed up with being the sensible one, the one who always did the right thing despite what she wanted to do. But strangely, until Logan had come back in her life, she'd never been tempted to do the wrong thing. It hadn't occurred to her. He obviously had a very bad effect on her.

Logan and Jack stared at each other, and it was a good job they weren't armed because neither of them looked happy. Time to pretend she was the nice, perfect person she used to be.

"Of course I'm okay," she said, plastering a smile on her stiff face. "Logan came to tell me what a nice lunch he had with Jenny."

"Oh. Well, do you want me to walk you to the station?"

Did she look like she needed someone to walk her to the station? Had she suddenly morphed into some fragile little woman who couldn't take care of herself? Something must have shown in her face, because Jack's eyes widened. "I mean as we're going the same way." He glanced between her and Logan. "That is, if we are…"

"No, go ahead. I'll be along in a minute."

He hesitated for a moment longer, and she glared.

He left.

Beside her Logan chuckled, and she looked at him sharply. His lips were curved into a smile. At least the tension seemed to have left him. "I think Jack just got a glimpse of my fantasy girl. Nice to know she's still there, hiding under all that sweetness and light."

"I am sweet."

"No, you're not. You just feel you have to pretend." He nodded to where Jack was disappearing down the road rather quickly. "I'm surprised he didn't stick around. I wouldn't leave my woman with someone like me."

"I'm not his woman. Whatever Jenny told you, there's nothing between us. We had one date two weeks ago, and I haven't been out with him since."

"Why?"

None of your goddamned business. But she kept the words inside. She was good at that, but it was getting harder and harder. Instead she took a deep, calming breath. "I didn't think it was right to see him while…" She wasn't sure how to end that.

"While you were fucking me."

Her lips tightened, but in fact, she rather liked the straight talking; she was sick of prevaricating over everything. "Exactly." Though that wasn't the only reason. She'd known Jack a long time, and she'd never had the urge to jump him, never had to curl her hands into fists to stop herself reaching out for him. Logan might not be right for her, but after what she had felt with him, she wouldn't settle.

She sighed. "Jack's a friend. I guess I'm realizing that if he was meant to be anything else, it would have happened by now."

"You mean like us. Five minutes after our eyes met, you were in my arms."

It had been like a blast of lightning. Lust at first sight. One look and she'd known she wanted him.

"Now all you need is to find a nice, suitable man who makes you feel like that."

"Good plan."

"Except, I don't think you like nice, suitable men. I don't think sensible gets your pussy all hot and wet." He leaned in closer. "I think Sergeant Abigail Parker has a secret hankering for bad boys."

She didn't answer. What was there to say? That her secret hankering was for just the one bad boy?

After a few seconds he stepped back and stood looking

down at her. "I actually came here today to tell you I was happy you'd found someone suitable. I told myself it was the right thing to do. But I find that I'm not capable of being quite that civilized yet." He gave her a feral smile. "And it would be a fucking lie. I don't want him touching you. And I certainly don't want him fucking you."

Again, she totally failed to think of anything intelligent to say.

She shook her head. She needed to go home before she caved and begged him to take her somewhere, anywhere, and touch her. More than touch her. She wanted to forget all the reasons why they shouldn't be together. Lose herself for a while. Loosen the strictures that wrapped around her life, so she could breathe again.

"But I'm working on it," he said. Reaching out, he stroked a hand down her cheek. "We'll work this out. And in the meantime, I'll keep out of your way."

He turned and walked away. Then he was gone, and she was left behind, staring after him, her heart aching.

Chapter Thirteen

She closed the door gently behind her, because otherwise she would have slammed it.

Jack was loitering in the station hallway, an expression of sympathy on his face. "You didn't get it?"

"No," she snapped. They had turned down her application for the detective bureau, hinting that she needed to be more circumspect with her personal life. A detective must be above reproach.

Assholes.

They had to be kidding.

And she'd sat there and taken it. Because what else could she do?

She couldn't believe it.

Well, unfortunately she could. But she was still seriously pissed off about it.

"I did warn you," said Jack. Her eyes narrowed on him. He didn't take the hint. "I told you hanging around with McCabe wouldn't do your career any good."

At his words, fighting mad turned into furiously angry.

She stalked toward him and stopped, hands on her hips. "Piss off, Jack. It's unfair and you know it. *And* it's a fucking double standard."

His eyes widened. He'd probably never heard her swear before.

"Those sanctimonious, hypocritical pricks in there had the nerve to tell me that a detective must be above reproach, when Brayden has been screwing around on his wife with PC Kinsley for the last three months. How circumspect is that?"

Jack glanced around. "Shh."

"What? Worried your boss will hear? It's not as if everyone doesn't already know."

"Come on. Let me give you a lift home. I've got the car today. You can apply again. You'll get in. Just…"

"Just what? Be more circumspect. Maybe you expect me to kick Logan out of Jenny's life. Would that help?" He shrugged. "Go away, Jack." Without waiting for him to answer, she whirled around and stalked away.

Logan sat, feet up on the desk, staring into space. There was probably something he should be doing, but he couldn't think what. And if there wasn't, he should be at home, not sitting in his office like some lovesick idiot. He'd gotten Abby's shift times off Jenny and knew them by heart. She wasn't working tonight. She'd probably be at home. Maybe he should go round, park outside her house, try and tempt her out.

He'd been so good, keeping his distance, but he was fed up with being good. It wasn't in his nature, and he had to work too hard.

But she couldn't come out, anyway. Her mother had moved in with her father, so Abby would be alone with Jenny.

Just as well.

The phone on his desk rang, and Logan picked it up. It was Mark, the bouncer working the door tonight. "Thought you might want to know, your Sergeant Parker just came in." The entire staff had been amused by Logan's new relationship with the law.

He frowned. He'd seen her briefly when he dropped Jenny off two nights ago, but other than that they hadn't spoken since he'd walked away a week ago. And it was killing him. So many times he'd thought about going to her. He wanted her back in his bed, or his truck, or up against the first convenient surface he could find. Now she had come to him, and excitement zinged in his blood. But it was after eleven. What was she doing out so late?

"Is she alone?"

"No, she's with two girlfriends. And boss, she's drunk. Made it clear she wasn't here to see you, just to party."

Drunk? Party? Neither sounded like Abby. What had happened? "Put her in the VIP section." He thought for a second, remembering what had happened last time she had been drunk in this club, and it wasn't going to happen with anyone else. "Don't let anyone near her, and I'll be right out."

He put the phone down and stared at it for a minute, then jumped to his feet, a grin tugging his lips.

She'd come to him.

Even if she denied it.

There were hundreds of other clubs in London if she wanted to party. No, whatever she said, it was him she wanted.

He made his way through the main room. The club was packed tonight, the lights dim, the air throbbing with the beat of the music. Carly was up on one of the podiums, looking classy in a black strapless dress and black heels. She gave an extra wiggle and blew him a kiss as he passed.

The bouncer opened the door to the VIP section as he approached. It was quieter in here, more subdued, the music lower, though the place was just as busy, and the small dance floor was packed. He saw Abby straight away and paused to study her. She was seated opposite two women, both blondes, in one of the plush red velvet booths that lined the walls. Mark stood in front of the little group, huge, arms folded across his chest, taking his scaring-off-potential-predators role very seriously.

She peered around Mark and caught sight of him, waggling her fingers. He moved forward, coming to a halt in front of her. Abby wasn't dressed to party, but in a black pantsuit and white shirt—the sort of thing she usually wore for work. Her face was free of makeup, her hair in its usual bun, although some curls had come free. He was guessing the party was a spur of the moment decision rather than a planned outing.

Logan nodded to Mark, and the bouncer headed off. Abby sat up straight, pushed her shoulders back, and smiled. "Good evening, Mr. McCabe."

His lips twitched. "Good evening." He looked to her friends. Was she going to introduce them, or was she going to try to pretend there was nothing between them?

Because he wasn't good enough.

But she waved a hand in their direction. "This is Melanie and Susannah. My friends." The waving hand wandered in his direction. "And this is Logan McCabe, bad boy, ex-con, and father of my daughter. And I"—she tapped herself on the chest—"am Abby, police sergeant and fantasy girl."

"Hi, Logan," said the one called Melissa, then she shrugged. "Sorry, we wanted to take her home, but she insisted. I think she wants to talk to you."

"No, I don't," Abby said. "Logan and I are best if we don't talk. If we talk things go bad. So, no, I don't want to talk to Logan." She thought for a moment. "I think I want to dance with Logan."

"Maybe we'll go get you a coffee first." Logan held out

a hand, and she slipped her palm into his and rose a little unsteadily to her feet. He turned back to her friends. "Thanks for looking after her. I'll send some drinks over." He tugged Abby after him, pausing by the bar on the way. The barman appeared immediately, and Logan told him to send over a bottle of champagne. He steered Abby toward the main room, intending to take her to the office, dose her with coffee, and find out where Jenny was.

She balked when she realized where they were going, digging in her heels. "No. I want to dance."

"Later."

Her eyes narrowed. "*Now*. And after that I want tequila. Lots of tequila."

The small dance floor was crammed. It would be an excuse to hold her close, which he needed because, the fact was, she was drunk, and he wasn't going to take advantage of that. But surely dancing was allowed within his somewhat hazy code of ethics.

"Okay, one dance." The music was slow, and he pulled her to him. Reaching up, she looped her arms around his neck and plastered her body against his. He slipped his hands beneath her jacket and dragged her even closer. They didn't dance, just swayed to the music, and for a brief time he shut himself off and stopped thinking, accepting the feeling of rightness. The restlessness that had been plaguing him fell away, and he closed his eyes, lowered his head, and breathed in the scent of her hair…lemons and flowers.

Her breasts were pressed against his chest and her head tucked into the curve where his neck met his shoulder. He went still as she kissed him, nuzzling his throat, and his cock stiffened. She must have felt it because she raised her head and peered up at him through her lashes. Her eyes were dark blue, a flush stained her cheeks, and she slowly licked her lips.

"Have you any more fantasies, Logan?"

He groaned. Maybe it was time to get her off the dance floor. "Why don't we go to my office, and I'll tell you all about them."

She flashed him a huge smile. "Excellent idea."

He spoke to one of the waitresses and ordered coffee in his office before ushering Abby out in front of him. This time she went without a fight. She flung herself on the leather sofa and kicked off her shoes, reached up behind her and pulled the remaining pins from her hair so it fell in a messy tangle down her back. His Ms. Prim and Perfect was coming undone in front of him. She wriggled out of her jacket and tossed it behind her, then patted the seat beside her. "Come and join me."

"I'll wait for the coffee."

"You don't want me anymore." She sounded woebegone.

"Not true. But you're drunk and it would be taking advantage."

She pouted. "I'm not that drunk. I'll show you." She got up, took a step, wobbled, and sat down again. "Oh."

"See? Drunk."

"I don't mind if you take advantage."

"You would tomorrow."

"Oh no, I wouldn't. But it's sweet—you're worried I won't respect you in the morning."

A knock sounded on the door and he went and collected the tray of coffee, kicking the door closed behind him. He brought the tray back, put it on the table, and sat down in the opposite corner of the couch. After pouring for them both, he handed her one, wrapping her fingers firmly around the mug. "Drink."

"Okay, maybe I am a little drunk. But I like it."

"Why are you drunk?"

She heaved her shoulders in a huge shrug. "Crap day."

"What happened? Is Jenny okay?"

"She's fine. I'd hardly be out getting drunk if she wasn't."

He exhaled. "No, of course not."

"She's at my mum's. Actually, my mum and dad's."

"So what went wrong today?"

She pushed out her lower lip in an exaggerated pout. "I didn't get my job. I wanted to be a detective. I've always wanted to be a detective, and they said I couldn't."

"You can't?"

She shook her head and swayed. "They said I needed to be more circumspect in my private life. But I'm Logan McCabe's fantasy girl, and apparently that's not very circumspect at all."

Shit. She was going to hold him responsible for this, and his good mood crashed. He'd fucked this up for her. He'd no doubt she would have made detective if he hadn't been on the scene.

"I don't blame you," she said as if reading his mind. She put her mug down and shuffled along the sofa until she was next to him then patted his arm. "I blame them. They're hypocrites and…and stupid people."

He chuckled. Stroking her hair back from her face, he rubbed the pad of his thumb over her cheek, the skin soft beneath his touch. "I'm sorry you didn't get your job. But maybe you were right. I'm not good enough for you."

"No, no, no." She leaned into him heavily. "It's me who's not good enough. You're perfect. Just perfect. If you weren't so perfect, I could be your fantasy girl, and when you've run out of fantasies, we could say good-bye and it wouldn't hurt. But you are, so I can't."

She wasn't making a lot of sense. He was as far from perfect as it was possible to be. He'd always been happy with the way he was. Now he wished he could be somehow better for her. Jesus, he was getting maudlin.

He rose to his feet and held out a hand. "Come on, I'll drive you home."

"I don't want to go home."

"You look tired. I'll tuck you up in bed."

She pursed her lips and thought for a moment before giving a small nod. "Okay." Her hand slid into his, and he tugged her up and wrapped an arm around her shoulder.

They were both quiet on the drive, though she turned to him at one point. "This isn't the way home."

"You can have a sleepover at mine. I don't want to leave you alone like this."

Her eyes narrowed. "Like what?"

He cast her a look, actually she was sobering up fast. "A little bit tipsy."

"So why can't you stay at my house?"

"Because Grunt doesn't like me to stay out all night."

"Fair enough." She closed her eyes and leaned her head back. Within seconds, her breathing changed, and she was asleep.

She hardly awoke as he led her to the spare room where she'd slept the last time she was here, but she balked at the door, blinking up at him. "No, I want to sleep in your room. You have to keep an eye on me."

He didn't argue. This might be the last chance he got to sleep with her, and while he had no intention of making love, not when she was so out of it, it would be good to hold her.

He didn't think he'd ever slept with a woman and not had sex. But Abby was different in so many ways.

Taking her hand, he led her down the hallway and into his room. She peered around, blinking slightly, then kicked off her shoes, crawled onto the bed, and burrowed under the bedspread. She punched the pillow once, snuggled her face in it, and was asleep in seconds. Logan stood looking down at her, just her head showing, her dark hair spread across the pillow.

Something warm uncoiled inside him, and for the first

time he acknowledged that his feelings for Abby went way beyond friendship. He just wasn't capable of putting those feelings into words.

Which was probably for the best. Because they made no difference. He was still no good for her.

All the same, he wanted to make things right for her, to go punch those sanctimonious bastards in the face, but that would hardly help. No, the only thing that would help is if he disappeared from her life, and that was impossible with Jenny between them. But he could distance himself. Avoid getting between Abby and her dreams.

What could *he* offer her? Fuck all, that's what.

Sighing, he scrubbed at his scalp, trying to shift the dull headache. He was a little puzzled that she didn't blame him for her not getting the job. That was a total turnaround from what she'd told him the night of Jenny's sleepover.

And she thought he was perfect. Hah. Perfect for what? He certainly wasn't perfect boyfriend material. And definitely not perfect husband material. A shudder ran through him at the thought. Look at Rory and his two marriages. The first had been, from all accounts, a trip to hell. His mother and father had lasted until six months after he'd been born, and Rory reckoned it had been the most miserable six months of his life. And while his second marriage had lasted much longer, and neither seemed inclined to seek a divorce, they spent the absolute minimum of time together, usually with the Atlantic Ocean between them. He'd thought Abby was like Judith, his father's second wife—uptight, prim and proper. But with Judith it went deep to the core. That was her true self. With Abby, it was a mere surface veneer, covering the real woman. But then, from what he'd gathered, she'd grown up thinking she had to show a perfect front to the world. Sort of the opposite of him, who'd grown up believing he had to show a tough, badass attitude.

Beneath that surface layer was the wild girl of his fantasy, but she was too ingrained in her ways to change now. She'd decided what she wanted in life and no way did he fit in. So he'd have to accept being Jenny's father and Abby's friend. From a distance.

Leaving her sleeping, he went downstairs and let Grunt out into the garden for a last sniff around. Once the dog was settled back in his bed, he returned to his room. He shut the door behind him, not quietly, but Abby didn't move. And she didn't stir when he went into the bathroom, or when he came out five minutes later, drying himself. He tossed the towel onto the chair by the bed, and slipped under the covers. Her back was to him and he wrapped an arm around her waist and pulled her close. His dick was happy to be there, but he ignored the way it stiffened against her ass.

Abby was the sort of woman you had for keeps. Unfortunately, he wasn't the sort of man who anyone kept long-term. He'd always known that. He'd screw up somehow. Better he backed off now and let her have a good life.

Just let him have this one last night.

He breathed in the warm scent of her, loving the sense of rightness, then closed his eyes and was asleep within minutes.

Chapter Fourteen

She didn't want to move. Abby woke up disorientated, with no clue where she was or how she'd gotten there. But she was warm, the bed was big and soft, and the body behind her hot and hard.

She snuggled backward, felt the twitch of Logan's cock against her ass. But she could tell from his breathing that he was still asleep, and she settled again, not wanting to wake him until she remembered how badly she'd behaved.

Peeking under the cover, she discovered she was almost fully dressed, so not that badly. Though as the memory filtered back, she realized it wasn't so much her *not* behaving badly as Logan behaving well. He'd been the perfect gentleman, refusing to take advantage of her. However much she'd begged him to. She burrowed her face in the pillow, but it smelled of Logan and only made her feel worse.

She hadn't wanted to go home the previous evening. When she'd left work, she'd phoned her mum, asked her to take Jenny for the night, and then called up her old school friends and asked if they would meet her. It had been a long time since they'd gotten together. She'd let her old friendships slide. It had been Mel and Sue who had organized her eighteenth birthday celebration, so they were sort of responsible for her relationship with Logan. Though "relationship" was probably the wrong word. Anyway, it had seemed appropriate to be with them last night.

She'd been so angry and frustrated. And for the first time she'd seen things from Logan's perspective, known what it was like for someone to look at you and make assumptions based on nothing more than what they saw on the surface. She was hanging around with Logan therefore she would make a crap detective. More likely it was because she'd said no to the chief inspector's advances when she first joined the force, and this was payback. He was using Logan as an excuse, and the others backed him up because that was the way things worked.

Well, she was fed up with it.

She'd always been good and look where that had gotten her. Nowhere.

Most of her life she'd gone out of her way to do the right thing. One little slip. Okay, maybe Logan wasn't so little—she pushed her ass back against his now truly impressive erection. And he wasn't really a slip. Whatever his appearance, or his past, Logan McCabe was a good man.

The reason she was running away was not because he was bad, but because she liked him too much. She winced as she remembered telling him last night that he was perfect. Well, perfect except for his total inability or wish to commit. And now, with what she knew of his background, she could understand that. But if he were a different sort of man, she'd be trying to make it work between them, trying to give Jenny a proper family.

Or if it were just her, she'd risk it, take him for however long she could have him, because she had an inkling that what they had was special, and she'd never find it with another man.

But she couldn't risk Jenny being hurt when her heart broke. How had she even let her heart get involved with his?

She sighed, and the hand around her waist tightened. Logan was awake.

"I can almost hear you thinking," he murmured against her ear.

She wriggled and managed to roll over so she was facing him. He was so beautiful her heart ached. His hair was loose around his shoulders, and this close she could make out the black line around the silver of his eyes. His cheeks were shadowed; he'd be scratchy when he kissed her. If he kissed her. The thought that he might never kiss her again, never touch her, was like a pain lodged deep inside her. But right now they were in bed together, and he was naked. Surely she deserved one last time. Then she would go back to being good.

She had to make it happen. Apart from the arm around her, he wasn't touching her now, and she needed him to touch her. Just once more and afterward, she'd find the strength to walk away.

He was returning her assessment. "How do you feel?" he asked. "Any aftereffects?"

She presumed he meant a hangover, and she gave a little shake of her head. "Fine. No aftereffects at all."

"Good. Come here"

The arm around her waist tightened and drew her closer, and at last his lips were on hers—soft at first, questioning. She pressed against him, opening her mouth, sliding her tongue along his lower lip, nipping him with her teeth, pushing inside. The glide of his tongue against hers turned her body hot and heavy, heat pooling in her belly, need pulsing between her thighs. Her clothes chaffed against her sensitive skin. She craved the feel of him naked against her, and she shifted restlessly.

He moved her so she was beneath him, cupping her face

in his hands and kissing her again, harder this time, taking control. "You're wearing too many clothes." He lifted his head to stare down into her face. His eyes held a question and a need that she guessed equaled her own. One she wouldn't deny.

"I know. Do you want to do something about that?"

"Yeah, I do."

He rested on one elbow, shoving the covers off them with his other hand, then studied her for a second, heat flaring in his eyes. He flicked open the buttons on her shirt, spreading the sides to reveal the white lace of her bra. As he stroked his knuckles over her nipples, spikes of pleasure raced along her nerves. He pushed the shirt from her shoulders, and she wriggled out of it, twisting to unfasten her bra.

"Christ, that is so pretty," he said, lowering his head to take one swollen nipple in his mouth, laving it with his tongue, sucking gently.

His lovemaking was unlike anything that had come before. Or maybe that was it—always before they'd had sex, fantastic mind-blowing sex, but this was so slow and gentle and intense. He moved to the other breast, kissing the tip, stroking his fingers over her until she was squirming beneath him, craving more.

His hand moved lower, opened the button at her waist, lowered the zipper on her pants, and she shoved them down, taking her panties with them and leaving her naked. "Much better." He cupped a hand between her thighs, and a groan escaped her.

"Is this another fantasy?" she asked.

His gaze lifted to her face. His expression was serious, his usual amusement absent. "No. This is real. This is you and me. Just once, and afterwards I'll leave you alone. I promise I won't hold you back. Now, I'm going to make love to you, slowly and completely, and you'll never forget the feel of me inside you."

She melted at his words, at the knowledge that he felt the difference, also. Maybe it was because they both recognized that this was the last time, and that they couldn't continue. The knowledge freed them to be themselves.

She traced the pattern of the tattoo on his chest, a red and black dragon, beautifully done, curling over his skin, breathing fire over his heart. Then she flicked a finger over the silver nipple ring and gave it a tweak. Moving lower, she trailed her fingers down the sleek, hard muscles of his stomach, twirling them in the silky hair that led to his groin. Finally, she wrapped her hand around the steely, burning length of his erection, squeezed, and heard his breath hitch.

His fingers moved between her thighs, slipping into the wetness, sliding over her sex, teasing her clit, pushing inside her. First one, then two, rubbing her inner walls so that everything tingled, and the desire in her belly tightened, growing heavy.

She needed him inside her, and she shifted restlessly.

"What do you want?" he murmured.

"You. Nothing else."

He pulled away for a moment while he rolled on a condom, then he moved over her body, balancing on one elbow as his other hand continued to move on her. The head of his cock pushed at the entrance to her body, and she lifted her hips, impaling herself on the thick, hard length of him. He filled her completely, and her eyes fluttered shut as she absorbed all the sensations swirling through her. She'd missed him so much. Missed this. How had she lived without him? How was she going to in the future?

Then he moved inside her, and she shoved everything from her mind. Everything but the feel of him, the slide of his body in hers. She wrapped her arms around him, hands on his ass, fingers digging into the satin skin, urging him closer, pulling him down to her so every inch of him pressed against her. He buried his head in the curve of her neck, kissing her throat, his chest rubbing her sensitive nipples, his hips pumping slowly into her.

She needed more, but she didn't want this to end, and she held herself still, trying to stave off the orgasm that hovered just within reach. Tension radiated from his body; he was close, and she wrapped him tighter, holding him still. He raised his head and gazed down into her face. She didn't want him to say anything to spoil the moment so she reached up and kissed him, stopping his words with her mouth and tongue. As he pressed down onto her, rotating his hips, the first sweet ripples of her orgasm shivered through her. He took control of the kiss as her back arched, and he ground softly against her until the pleasure rolled over her like a tidal wave, swallowing her up, dragging her under.

I love you.

The words echoed through her mind, but she kept them locked inside, not wanting to scare him off. She lost herself for a while, was vaguely aware of him coming inside her, the press of his body on hers, the taste of him still in her mouth.

Finally he went still, gave her one last kiss, rolled off her and onto his side, pulling her with him so she lay with her back flush against him, his hand cupping her breast.

She was hovering on the edge of sleep when she caught his whispered words against her skin.

"Good-bye, fantasy girl."

Her heart ached and her eyes pricked, but she held herself very still, and finally she slept.

When she awoke, she was alone.

The fantasy was over.

Time to find a way back to real life.

Chapter Fifteen

Josh looked rough. Worse than rough, and Vito was no better.

Logan was guessing he wasn't the only one stressing about their life-changing vows, regretting the decisions they had made while bobbing around in that lifeboat, puking and contemplating dying.

Coming face to face with death had a way of changing a man, making him think about how things might have been different. But the problem was you couldn't rely on your brain to work the way it should at times like those. Couldn't rely on the decisions you made being the right ones. The sensible ones. But then, since when had he been interested in being sensible?

"Things to do before you die. Whose fucking idea was that anyway?" Josh said, throwing back the whiskey and slamming his glass down on the table. Logan reached across and filled it from the bottle in front of him and topped off his own at the same time. Vito's was still full.

"I think it was yours," Logan said.

"Never. Not in a million years would I have put myself in

this situation. Besides, I had a broken leg at the time, and two broken ribs. Why would the two of you listen to a man who was in pain and obviously not thinking straight?"

"I take it things are not going well with your…wife?"

"Things are going shit. And I don't want to talk about it. I just want to drink."

"How about you?" Logan asked Vito.

"I'm not drinking. I have a gut feeling that drunk, I will make a decision that I will later regret. So I'm staying sober."

"Give us some good news," Josh said. "How's your fantasy girl? Everything you dreamed of?"

Everything and more.

But he kept the words to himself. It did no good thinking about that. Eventually, the pain would go away.

An image of Abby flashed in his mind, so prim and proper, followed by another of her coming apart for him so sweetly. So fucking gorgeous. He drained his glass, the whiskey a warm buzz in his head. "Nothing like I remembered."

"Sorry, mate."

The Abby of his dreams had been a fabrication. The real thing was so much more genuine. Of more substance. A good person, much too good for the likes of him. He shrugged. "Some things should be left alone." But then he would never have found Jenny. However much pain he was experiencing right now, he wouldn't want her not to be in his life. She'd changed him. Always before, he'd run away from commitment, but with Jenny there *was* no running away. Maybe if he'd known her earlier, from when she was a baby, he might have turned out a different man, a better man, and he'd have been able to give Abby the life she deserved.

"Seems like we're all fucked royally," Vito said.

"Yup." Josh agreed. "Let's get pissed."

Vito took a deep breath. "Fuck this." He picked up his drink, swallowed the contents in one go and pushed his empty glass toward Logan. "Fill it up."

Three hours later, Logan watched them lurch from the bar. The club had closed an hour ago, and Mark was driving the pair back to where they were staying.

The bottle of whiskey was empty, as was the second.

Maybe he should feel better that it wasn't only his love life that had turned to shit, but he found himself wishing that the other guys could have found their dreams, even if he hadn't. Christ, maybe he was turning into a nice guy.

He needed tequila. Abby had tasted of tequila that very first night they had met. Pushing himself up, he wobbled, resting his hand on the table to steady himself. Abby should be here to see this. Get her own back for last night. Maybe he should call her.

But no, they weren't seeing each other again, except for with Jenny, or to talk about Jenny. He could do this. He lurched to the bar and banged on it. A waitress was filling up the shelves. She glanced up, her eyes widening. "What can I get you, boss?"

"Tequila."

She glanced around as if looking for someone to give her permission. When no one materialized, she shrugged and got down a bottle and a glass. She made to pour it, but he held out his hand. When she hesitated he snarled, "Give me the goddamned bottle, Angie."

He took it back to his office and threw himself onto the sofa, clutching the tequila to his chest. He'd made love to Abby for the first time on this very sofa. He'd woken up here the morning after and known he'd found something special.

Then he'd fucked up.

Like he always did.

He should never have let her run. He should have taken her home, stuck to her like glue, and maybe things would have turned out differently. He would have turned out different.

Now it was too late, and he had to let her go.

He unscrewed the top from the tequila, sniffed it, brought it to his mouth, but changed his mind and lowered the bottle again. Even if he wasn't good enough for Abby, he was going to do his best to be a good father, a responsible father. And that didn't involve drinking himself into oblivion at three in the morning, however much he wanted the pain to go away.

He should go home, but half an hour later he was still lying on the sofa, clasping the bottle to his chest, when Rory slipped through the door. He crossed the room and stood looking down at Logan, then he tugged the bottle from his fingers. He shook his head as he placed the tequila on the table.

"Angie," he called out, and the waitress must have been loitering just outside, because she peered around the door.

"Yes, boss?"

Logan swung his legs around so he was sitting upright. His head hurt, and he pressed a finger to his forehead while he cast her a disgusted glance. "Did you call my dad on me?"

"Of course she did," Rory said. "Get me a scotch, darling, and a jug of coffee for the boy."

She gave him a quick smile and disappeared. Logan eyed his father. "I'm not a boy."

"So stop behaving like one." Rory sat at the far end of the sofa and studied him, head cocked to one side. "Though maybe you needed this. You did have your somewhat wild youth cut short. So which particular sorrows are you drowning tonight?"

"I'm not drowning any sorrows."

Angie came back at that moment, placed a pot of coffee and a mug in front of him and a large scotch in front of Rory. She poured the coffee and backed away. "I'll be leaving now."

"Okay, we'll lock up." Rory sipped his scotch and watched him for a moment. "How's Jenny?"

"Fine."

"And her mother?"

Logan flashed a look at his father, but Rory's face was expressionless. "Also fine."

"So are you two seeing each other?"

Nosy bastard. "Of course we are. We saw each other when I collected Jenny a couple of days ago." He picked up his coffee, hoping the conversation was over. No such luck.

"Drink your coffee," Rory said. "I want you sober before we have this conversation, because I'm not saying it twice."

Logan stifled the urge to storm out, since that would be childish. Besides, part of him was interested in what his father had to say. Rory had never been in the habit of dishing out parental advice—not to him anyway. He drank his coffee, poured himself another, and drank that. By the time he'd finished the second, his head was clearing. He put down the mug and leaned back, staring Rory in the face. His dad didn't look away. "Say what twice?"

"How do you feel about Abby?"

Not what he was expecting. "It doesn't matter what I feel."

"And why is that?"

"Because she's too fucking good for me."

Rory raised an eyebrow. "Really?"

"Really." Anyone could see that. "So I am doing the noble thing and backing off. She can find a nice man and have a nice life."

"Bullshit"

"Bullshit?" Of course it wasn't bullshit.

Rory slammed his empty glass down then stared him in the eye. "At least have the guts to admit that you're shit-scared."

He frowned. "I am?"

Rory ignored the question. "And if you're not scared it's because you're being a total pussy and playing it safe. Maybe you're not good enough for her. Or maybe you're too good. She's certainly not the sort of woman I would have expected you to fall for."

"She's perfect."

"Of course she is...*not*. No one is perfect. Not me, not you, and certainly not Abby."

He searched for a flaw in that statement. "Declan was perfect."

"And look where that got him. Close to imploding."

"True." Logan poured another cup of tepid coffee and gulped it down. He had a hunch his dad was right, and he did need to be sober for this conversation. "Don't you think it's a little late to start handing out fatherly advice?" he asked Rory as he placed the empty mug back on the table.

"Probably. With you I never tried. Never thought I had the right. Besides, you were always a contrary little brat. Tell you one thing and it was a guarantee you'd go the other way." He grinned. "Actually, I liked that in you. You're like me. Too much like me. Which doesn't mean I have to sit by and watch you make the same mistakes."

"It's not a mistake. She wants different things. She wants a good life and a man who'll stick by her and provide a stable home for Jenny." And how he fucking hated the thought of some other man doing that.

"And you can't do that?"

The question stopped him short. Could he? A shiver of fear ran through him. What if he did all that, offered her everything, all of him, forever, and she still walked away? How long would it take her to realize that he really wasn't good enough? If he gave her everything and she dumped him, would he ever recover?

For God sake, he hardly had a good track record.

At least this way he was getting out before he got in too deep.

Though who was he kidding? He was as deep as he could go.

"Like I said. Why not fucking admit it?" Rory cut through his thoughts. "You're shit-scared. You think if you let yourself fall in love, eventually Abby will dump you like your mother did. Isn't that the case?"

The words so mirrored his own thoughts that his mouth dropped open. Rory let out a short, humorless laugh. "I married your mother because of you. She was never what you might call lovable, but she was fucking gorgeous. It's not a basis for marriage. I married Judith because she could give me what I needed—respectability. But never love. I understand why—I never considered I deserved love and believe me, in my case I had good reason. I did some fucked up crap when I was young. But you..." He ran a hand through his hair. "I've never been good at this shit." He took a deep breath. "What I'm trying to say is that you are in no way to blame for the stuff that went down when you were a kid. Just as I suspect Abby is in no way to blame for how she's turned out."

"She's fucking perfect," he growled.

Rory grinned. "Of course she is. So you'll back off and let her find someone equally perfect? Hell, maybe you can be a fucking bridesmaid at their wedding."

"Bastard." He exhaled loudly.

"How much of a coward are you, son?" Rory stood up. "Enough from me. Except—don't fuck this up. I like her. And anyway, now that we've got Jess in the family we need someone nice to balance it up."

Logan watched as he walked away.

Okay, step one. Accept that he was, in actual fact, shit-scared. Scared that he'd offer himself up and she'd find him wanting. That he'd fall in love...

As the word crossed his mind, he had a revelation, almost equal to the one he'd had in that boat when his life had flashed in front of him and he'd realized he might die without ever setting eyes on his fantasy girl again.

It was too late.

Way too late.

Because he was already in love with her. She was no longer a fantasy; she was his one-time chance at a real-life happy ever after.

Only if he had the guts to go after her, and if he was willing to take the risk and put his heart on the line.

For a brief moment he considered changing. Making himself into the sort of man she'd always wanted. A suit and a tie. A sensible car and a haircut. But he quickly banished the thought. Besides, Abby thought he was perfect, she'd told him so. She might have been drunk at the time, but weren't people supposed to tell the truth when they were drunk?

Hell, he wasn't anywhere close to perfect. But maybe they were perfect for each other.

And he knew where he was going to approach her. Right in front of her upstanding friends and colleagues. Time for her to decide what really mattered, and if there was any place for him in her perfect life.

All or nothing.

Abby was working at her desk, willing the time away so her shift would end. She longed to get away from here and be alone while she put herself back together again. While she did her best to forget how good Logan McCabe could make her feel, put him in a box and label it "Jenny's dad" and somehow convince herself he could never be anything more.

She truly believed that deep down, Logan cared for her, but it wasn't enough. If it had merely been that he didn't want to commit because he liked playing the field, she might have tried to persuade him otherwise. But it was much more than that.

Over the long days, she'd relived all their time together, along with what she knew of his past. And she'd finally got it. He was scared. Scared of commitment. Scared of loving someone and having that love thrown back in his face.

And really, it was hardly surprising considering his crappy childhood and his horrible mother. Rory probably hadn't helped either. She was just glad Logan had opened his heart to Jenny. That must have been an act of courage for him.

Now she was going to make it easier for him and take a step back. Logan was Jenny's father and that was all. As for her and Logan, she would maintain her distance and ensure they were never alone. Eventually, she would stop hurting.

And she'd make it clear here at work that there was nothing between the two of them except Jenny. She'd be so circumspect they wouldn't be able to fault her, and the next time a vacancy came up in the detective bureau, she would get the job. That might be some compensation.

Logan had been a glitch in her road to perfection, but if she worked hard enough she could get back on track.

But she didn't want to be back on track.

And she didn't want to be perfect.

She wanted Logan. There was a constant ache in her heart because she couldn't have him. She rested her forehead against the cool metal of the desk and closed her eyes.

A door opened and the sound of raised voices drifted down the corridor. Abby lifted her head, her breath hitched, and a frown formed between her brows.

Was that Logan's voice? If it was, he didn't sound happy.

What was here doing here?

Had he been arrested for something?

The thought flickered through her mind, and she tossed it out. No way. Logan was a good man. And besides, he had that whole calm-in-the-face-of-adversity thing.

So if he hadn't been arrested, what was he doing here?

Without conscious thought, she was on her feet and heading down the corridor. She pushed open the swinging doors leading into the reception area, her gaze locked on Logan's back, her heart speeding up. She gave herself a little shake, dragged her gaze away, and tried to make sense of the scene in front of her.

The sergeant on duty had a bewildered expression on his face as though not entirely sure what was going on—so she wasn't alone. Jack stood in front of the desk, facing Logan, and a whole crowd of uniformed and plain clothes police were watching them avidly.

She turned her attention back to Logan, and the ache in her chest eased a little, as though just being in the same room was enough to banish the pain. A smile tugged at her lips, and she forced it away.

Distance.

"Sergeant Parker." She jumped as someone spoke from behind her. Her boss stood with his eyes narrowed on her, his hairy brows drawn together. "What's going on?"

"I really don't know, sir."

At the sound of her voice, Logan spun around, and for a second she drank him in. Today he was all bad-boy menace in black leather, his hair pulled back, stubble darkening his cheeks, eyes slightly bloodshot and...she looked lower...he had a huge bunch of crimson roses clutched in his hand. A little flicker of hope sparked to life inside her.

Jack edged in her direction, and Logan turned to him with a frown, looming over the other man, a sneer on his face. Oh God, she hoped he wasn't going to punch him. "You don't get to have her, Jack. And you know why? Because she's mine."

A little thrill of pleasure shot along her nerves.

"I think we'll let Abby decide that," Jack said.

"So let her."

"I really don't think this is the place—"

Logan was bristling with barely leashed menace. He really didn't like Jack. Time to jump in and keep the peace. She hurried out of the doorway and all eyes turned her way.

Logan took a step toward her, his gaze fixed on her face, his expression solemn, a question in his eyes. She moved toward him as though she couldn't help herself, ignoring their audience because something was happening here. Something more important than any of her colleagues' opinions.

Everyone else faded into the background as her whole attention focused on Logan. She could see the fear in his eyes but also his resolve. He'd come for her, to the one place he hated. He was exposing his fears totally, and the love and hope she'd been holding tight inside blossomed, flooding her system with warmth. But also with a need to protect him, keep him safe, and somehow convince him that if he took the chance on her she'd never let him down.

They stopped only inches apart. He stroked a finger down her cheek, and a shiver ran through her. "You look tired, fantasy girl."

"I haven't been sleeping too well."

"Me, neither. You want to help me with that?"

"Every night if you want me to."

He exhaled, some of the tension easing from his body. "I can't promise not to screw up, but if you give me a chance, I'll do my best for you and Jenny. I'll never purposefully let you down."

"I know."

"I've got to be honest—I'm scared of messing up, but I'm more scared of not being part of your lives. I need you. Both of you. Everything is meaningless without you."

God, she wanted to hug him. "We need you too, Logan."

Closing the final distance between them, he reached for

her, crushing his bouquet of flowers between them. He gave her a quick smile, then turned and shoved the roses at Jack. "Hold on to these. I'll need them in a minute."

Jack opened his mouth, but no sound came out, then she forgot all about him as Logan cupped her face with both hands and stared down into her eyes. The room and everyone but Logan faded away.

"Kiss me," she muttered. When he was too slow, she curled her fingers in the silky hair at the back of his neck, tugged him down, and parted her lips beneath his. His hands shifted to her hips and he lifted her so her feet were off the floor, and he kissed her until her head swam.

The sound of stamping feet and wolf whistles finally broke through the haze fogging her mind.

"Way to go, sergeant!"

Logan pulled back slightly, lowered her to the floor, and rested his forehead against hers. "Hardly circumspect, sarge," he murmured against her skin.

"Bugger circumspect," she replied.

He chuckled then released her, stepped back, and stretched a hand behind him. "Flowers, Jack."

As Jack handed them to him, he gave Abby a rueful smile and a shrug.

Logan held out the roses. She took them and buried her nose in the fragrant petals, breathing in the heavy perfume. Finally she lifted her head and found him watching her, a hot, hopeful expression in his silver eyes.

Ask me. Ask me.

He put his hand into his pocket and pulled something out. Her heart hitched then started thumping fast and hard. Her gaze flashed from the ring in his hand to his face, and his eyes were filled with emotion so clear that when the words came they held no surprise. "I love you."

She didn't have to think about her reply. "I love you too."

A cheer went up around the room.

Logan exhaled loudly, and the last of the tension oozed out of him. He'd clearly been in no way sure of her. "Good."

"Is this one of your fantasies?" she asked.

"No, this is as real as it gets." He took a deep breath. "So, Sergeant Abigail Parker, will you marry me?"

She held out a shaking hand, and he slipped the ring on her finger. "I will."

Epilogue

"I hate bloody boats," Logan muttered.

They were honeymooning on the island of Sicily, staying in the extremely luxurious villa of one of Logan's friends, Vittorio D'Ascensio, whom she'd met at the wedding a week ago. The yacht was also Vito's, and they'd taken it out for the day. The sea was calm, but even so, Logan's face held a tinge of green.

"We didn't have to come," she said.

"I wanted to show you." He held on to the railing with one hand and waved the other out toward the rocky shoreline. "That's where the ship went down. We were right here when I decided that no way was I going to die without finding my fantasy girl."

She moved to stand beside him at the rail, wrapping her arm around his waist as she gazed out over the flat sea. The water was a deep turquoise blue, reflecting the clear sky above them, and the sun was hot on her back. "So if you'd never gone on the boat, you would never have come to find me?"

He turned to peer down at her, a lazy smile curling his

beautiful lips. "I think I would have come to find you in the end. The life and death thing just nudged me in the right direction."

A shiver ran through her as she realized how close he had come to dying. They might never have met again. The idea seemed inconceivable. "Nothing like the thought of dying to make you realize what you really want."

"Exactly. And I wanted my fantasy girl."

"You have her."

"Actually, I have my fantasy woman." He lowered his head and kissed her neck, sending ripples of desire spreading through her. Then he nipped her skin. "So why don't we head back to solid ground."

"Are we going to do the fantasy thing?" Her body tingled at the thought. She'd even packed her handcuffs, because she'd never been able to get that particular image out of her mind. Maybe today…

"I don't need fantasies anymore," Logan said. "I have the real thing."

"Aw."

He grinned. "Okay, perhaps I still have a few left."

"Enough for a lifetime?"

"More than enough."

She leaned across and kissed him slowly and thoroughly. "My fantasy guy."

Acknowledgments

To everyone at Entangled Publishing, but especially my wonderful editor, Candace Havens, for all her great comments, edits and perseverance. And to all the great women at Passionate Critters for reading my stories and letting me know what they really think. And finally, to my husband Rob, who puts up with me, and encourages me, and does a great job of hiding it when he's totally fed up with me vanishing into my imaginary worlds and filling the house with imaginary people.

About the Author

Nina Croft grew up in the north of England. After training as an accountant, she spent four years working as a volunteer in Zambia, which left her with a love of the sun and a dislike of nine-to-five work. She then spent a number of years mixing travel (whenever possible) with work (whenever necessary) but has now settled down to a life of writing and picking almonds on a remote farm in the mountains of southern Spain.

Nina writes all types of romance, often mixed with elements of the paranormal and science fiction.

And if you'd like to have learn about new releases sign up for Nina's newsletter here: http://eepurl.com/rZ5rz

www.ninacroft.com

Break Out

Deadly Pursuit

Death Defying

Temporal Shift

Blood and Metal

Flying Through Fire

Malfunction

The Order series

Bittersweet Blood

Bittersweet Magic

Bittersweet Darkness

Bittersweet Christmas

The Order Boxed Set

Melville Sisters series

Operation Saving Daniel

Betting on Julia

Beyond Human series

Unthinkable

Unspeakable

Uncontrollable

Blackmailed by the Italian Billionaire

The Spaniard's Kiss

If you love sexy romance, one-click these steamy
Brazen releases...

WET AND RECKLESS
a Private Pleasures novel by Samanthe Beck

Aspiring singer/songwriter Roxy Goodhart's latest mistake is a doozy, involving a lying ex-manager, a dire lack of cash, and a teensy bit of grand larceny. Landing in the long, strong, entirely too tempting arms of the law is no way to keep a low profile. Taking an apartment puts her under orderly West Donovan and in his path every day. Testing his impressive reserve is beyond reckless, but she'd love to test it...all...night...long.

HER MARINE NEXT DOOR
a novel by Aliyah Burke

My sexy neighbor Parker Jax isn't my type—he's covered in tats, rides a motorcycle, and his parties keep me up all night. I'm a quiet artist. He's a rowdy marine. I've got a broken heart. He probably doesn't have a heart. Then, the jerk has to go and help me, and now I owe him. And when a woman shows up with a kid, knocking on his door, Parker's calling in the debt...

Seducing the Fireman
a Risky Business novel by Jennifer Bonds

Firefighter Jackson Hart is back in Brooklyn and on the hunt for the girl who's kept him burning for ten long years. The girl he left, in a total prick move, without saying goodbye. He's determined to make it up to her, but Becca's not ready to forgive and forget. Good thing Jax isn't the kind of man to give up when he wants something. And he *always* gets what he wants.

Playing with Trouble
a Sydney Smoke/Credence Crossover novel by Amy Andrews

Australian rugby pro Cole Hauser is ready for some peace and anonymity. The plan is perfect—until he discovers he's roomies with single mom Jane Spencer and her kid. While she's rehabbing the house in hopes it will put her business on the map, he's knee-deep in kid activities—and unexpectedly loving it. The situation is temporary, so it should be easy to say goodbye. However, it doesn't take long for them to realize they've borrowed a whole lot of trouble…but trouble never felt this good.